Paging Dr. Breakup

Paging Dr. Breakup

Yukon Valley, Alaska Hospital Novel

Jillian David

TULE
PUBLISHING

Chapter One

DEIRDRE STEEN HURRIED down the hall, her caffeinated lifeline clutched in a lidded tumbler this chilly Monday morning. She straightened the casual black blazer layered over her sky-blue blouse. As the chief nursing officer for Yukon Valley Hospital, Deirdre didn't need to hurry.

That said, avoidance was a powerful motivator. She'd seen the on-call schedule. Therefore, she needed to hurry.

Deirdre toyed with the hem of the blazer.

As long as she didn't go near the ED, everything would be fine.

"Morning, Billy," she called out to the middle-aged front desk staff member who somehow managed to hear every bit of gossip that came through the doors of Yukon Valley Hospital. The Alaska interior might have reduced connectivity compared with urban areas, but the internal communication both in the town and within the hospital flowed at light speed.

"Good morning, Deirdre," he replied with a quick smile. "You're really moving this morning. Off to meet someone?"

Precisely what she wasn't doing. "Just getting my steps in early."

The late March sun streamed through the bank of tall

windows near the reception area of the hospital. The days might be longer, but the sun wasn't yet strong enough to melt the piles of snow that had been pushed to the back of the hospital parking lot. With the gravel and asphalt surface visible in several spots, that meant mud season was almost here. Deirdre groaned to herself, already imagining the annual mess the hospital's environmental services staff would once again tackle.

Like waking up from a cold winter's sleep, the entire town seemed on the verge of breakup season, the time when the Yukon River was released from its icy prison and began flowing once again. Hell, Yukon Valley had an entire festival dedicated to the river turning from solid to liquid.

A nasty shudder ran through her. After her parents' bush plane crash onto unstable ice four years ago, Deirdre refused to venture onto the frozen river, even in the safest conditions. Ice fishing on twelve inches of rock-solid ice in the dead of winter a few feet from shore? Nope.

So, the idea of celebrating the Yukon River becoming a relentless force of deadly, crushing ice floes was a definite *no thank you.*

Passing the doctors' lounge door, she blinked when a sunbeam blinded her, a split second before she crashed into a solid wall of human being.

"Oh my God!" she exclaimed.

Her mouth dropped open in soundless horror as a fresh coffee stain spread over a gray Patagonia vest. Droplets absorbed into seafoam green scrub sleeves. She glanced at the speckled once-white lanyard and followed it down to the employee photo. Oh, no. Of all the people.

Calvin Garrett.

Damn it.

"Whoa there." Calvin took her upper arm in a steadying grip. Then they both froze. "Deirdre? Is it really you?"

For a solid five seconds, Deirdre's world tilted as she stared at steel-gray eyes she never expected to see again. Calvin. Her childhood friend. Her husband's childhood friend. The only person in Yukon Valley who she wanted to avoid, standing right in front of her. Holding her upright.

The quick furrow of his brows and a mischievous smirk took her right back to high school where she, her future husband Elijah, and Calvin had all been thicker than thieves. Those were good times. The time before Calvin left. The time before she married Elijah.

The time long before Elijah had gotten sick.

Calvin's face had changed over the years, giving him a weathered, harder, but still handsome appearance. Nowadays, his dark, close-cut hair had sparkles of gray at the temples. His secure hold and his lean frame reminded her that some things didn't change.

Acutely aware of Billy watching with rapt attention from the front desk, his hand mere inches away from the reception desk phone, ready to dial a friend to share this tasty interaction with the entire staff, Deirdre gave a polite laugh. "Hey, it's great to see you, Calvin." Crap, that came out way too corporate.

She craned her neck. His six-foot-two height hadn't changed over the years.

"I heard you'd be helping us this spring while you were in town helping your folks. Glad to hear that your dad is doing better." She stepped back, and his hands dropped to his sides. "Again, *oof*. Sorry about your … outfit."

With a shrug, he mock-whispered, "First of all, did you know the scrubs are free in this place?" Then he grinned, transforming from a man in his late thirties to the cheeky and confident high school senior he used to be. "Second of all, you don't have to be an administrator for my benefit, Deirdre. It sounds like you're going to assign an AIDET patient communication module for me to complete on the spot." He huffed. "What about *hi, Cal, how about a hug?*"

Denying the urge to scan for an audience, she kept her gaze on Cal. "Ahem. I have it on good record that you already completed your training modules during onboarding. And I'd give you a hug, but you appear to have coffee all over you." She sniffed and gestured with the empty tumbler at her outfit. "Um, I have my clean work clothes on."

"That's an excuse." Not exactly a question, but not a statement.

Heat climbed her neck and cheeks. The years-long urge to sink into his embrace caught her completely off guard.

Hey, this might be a rural facility in the middle of nowhere, but Yukon Valley Hospital is still a place of business. As an administrator, she needed to maintain decorum and lead by example.

The smile on Calvin's face fell. Her palms sweated. Decorum be damned. Deirdre was also very human. Calvin was an old friend. Covering the delay, she said, "You threw me for a minute. Here you go." She opened her arms wide, pushing past a zip of fear, and something else undefinable that made her arms shake.

"Well, that's better," he said, drawing her in for a warm, firm hug. They embraced for a few seconds longer than colleagues should.

Giving a friendly pat on his back, more to make herself let go, she said, "Great seeing you, Calvin."

"You already said that." He took a step back, arms falling to his sides once more. His quick, wry smile disappeared, replaced by a thoughtful, more intense expression.

Deirdre stammered beneath the evaluation, "So, how are you getting settled in?"

His gaze narrowed as he shifted to professionalism. Good. He gave a quick nod. "This is my first shift since coming back to town. Figure it's like riding a bicycle, except in emergency medicine, sometimes the bicycle is on fire and sometimes you're riding four bicycles at once. Which are all on fire."

"And sometime all of the bicycles have flat tires and brakes not working!" Deirdre laughed out loud, surprising herself with how light those few seconds felt. "*Phew*, you described every single day of my job. We never know what life throws at us, am I right?"

Concern creased the weathered lines of his face. She could imagine him using this exact compassionate expression when breaking bad news or discussing complex medical decisions.

He tugged at the fleece vest pocket. "You know I'm

really sorry about everything that happened with Elijah. And then with your folks. All of that had to have been a lot to handle."

It was a lot to handle without her longtime friend Calvin present. A lump ached in her throat. Her assessment was unfair. Her brother, Maverick, had supported her. They had supported each other. Besides, Calvin had visited Elijah in hospice before he had passed, and he had sent flowers after her parents' death.

She blinked several times and locked her jaw until her teeth ached. Whatever it took to maintain control in a public and professional space, Deirdre would do it. "You're right. I really miss them."

"Me too. I sometimes imagine paddling with Elijah, running rapids and coming up with plans to fix everything wrong in the world." His Adams apple bobbed a few times and then he cleared his throat. "So, lots of memories." He smiled. "Would you be opposed to catching up with an old friend over dinner sometime?"

The tight knot in her throat eased. Warmth flowed through Deirdre's limbs, chased by a flicker of fear. Dinner with Calvin. Their history. Her buried feelings.

Even though she stood on solid ground, his invitation triggered a sensation like stepping onto a frozen river with zero confidence that the crackling ice would hold her weight.

Stop it. They were old friends. Besides, maybe it would be good for her to talk about Elijah. Share memories and laugh or cry at stories. Expressing emotions was a tall order. If avoiding feelings had become a habit, then maintaining emotional distance from everyone and everything was her lifestyle. But this was Calvin.

Deirdre felt her head bobbing. "Sure, I wouldn't mind grabbing a bite to eat. We can reminisce about old times. I know you're busy with Bruce and Aggie these days, so if you want, email or text me some times that work for you."

He pinned her with another sharp glance, then one corner of his mouth rose. "Sounds like you're putting me off. Have your people call my people, and they'll send a meeting invite? Should I coordinate with your administrative assistant?"

Busted. Holding up a hand, she stammered, "It's not like that." Actually, it was. "I just know that my busy schedule and your busy schedule may not easily line up. But yes, we will find time." Or find excuses not to have time.

Busy. Understatement of the year. Deirdre did her part to keep the hospital running by cobbling staff together. She pitched in on shifts as a last resort, begged staff for help, and kept advertising the unfilled positions. In addition, she helped her brother Mav run their family's lodge business. Within the past month or so, the recent discovery of potential minerals on their property meant that she also wanted to figure out how to monetize that find. Or rather, prevent others from monetizing it first.

The most pressing issue? Deirdre needed to survive the Breakup Festival next month.

Calvin glanced at her face before looking toward Billy, who was doing his level best to appear busy doing nothing, despite leaning toward them with his head cocked.

Then Calvin lightly brushed his fingertips over her fore-arm. "It's great to see you, and it will be great to catch up." He tugged at his vest and shrugged. "Sounds like I should go change before the first patient thinks I'm a sloppy mess."

"Yikes. Well, at least you smell like coffee. There are many other stains you can get in the hospital that would be so much worse."

His warm, baritone laugh that Deirdre hadn't heard in so many years dredged up a deep sense of conflict.

Later.

Now wasn't the time to be dealing with feelings. Not at work. She had a unit manager meeting to lead in ten minutes and apparently a dinner to schedule with Calvin.

Chapter Two

DEIRDRE STEEN. LESS than one minute of physical contact—that was all it took to encapsulate why Calvin had stayed away from Yukon Valley.

The simple acts of steadying her with his hands and holding her in his arms hit Cal harder than paddling straight into a hidden rock in class IV rapids. His stability shifted, and he had to quickly regain his balance.

He knew he'd eventually run into her at the hospital, but nothing had prepared him for those bright blue eyes twinkling up at him—at times crinkling with laughter or sad.

He peered at her retreating frame. Deirdre had more curves than back in high school. Her beauty had evolved along with her confidence. Time, care, and stress had etched faint lines of character and hard-won wisdom on her features. Her attractive face, framed by jaw-length chestnut hair, served as a testament to both survival and kindness.

He glanced over to Billy at the front desk, who to his credit, pretended to work, randomly punching the numbers on the unanswered phone in front of him. Like most folks in this area, Cal knew Billy from years ago. He had graduated high school when Cal was in middle school, but Billy's reputation for extreme nosiness remained legend in school and in the community. Now? That guy had the perfect job to suit his talents.

Now there was a story of how Deirdre and Cal had literally crashed into each other and made awkward small talk. Yeah, zero chance that tale wouldn't make it to every ear in the community by dinnertime.

He eyed Billy, who grinned like a Cheshire cat.

Make that lunchtime.

He waved at Billy and walked into the emergency department, en route to snag some spare scrubs and change clothes in the on-call room.

Amberlyn, one of the nurses on shift in the ED, intercepted him. "What happened to you?"

"Me versus Deirdre Steen's coffee mug. The mug won. Who knew coffee is more effective if it's taken by mouth rather than applied topically." He gestured toward the mocha-scented brown spots speckling his vest and scrubs.

She giggled. "The Steens seem to have an uncanny habit of bumping into doctors these days. Must be fate."

Cal shook his head. His parents had filled him in on all the details of how Deirdre's brother Maverick Steen and Dr. Lee Tipton became romantically involved – with the help of hospital staff and community members. Turned out Cal's parents played an unorthodox part in the mischief. To hear Pop tell it, it was Pop's fake-patient acting job that finally forced Maverick and Dr. Lee to declare their intentions. Their love was good news for the couple, the hospital, and the community. In this small town at the end of the world, people relished a happy ending.

The bad news? If Amberlyn's wolflike smile was any indication, the local matchmaking team had moved on to their next project. He gulped.

"Deirdre?" Her avid stare terrified him as she tapped her chin. "Oh yeah. I can see it. You two would make a cute couple."

Not if he had any say in it. Time to nip this rumor in the bud. He held up his hands. "No. We are good friends from all the way back in elementary school."

Her brows shot up. "So, you know about her husband being gone?"

He threw as much weight and sadness into his next words. Anything to shut down this line of questioning and well-meaning meddling. "Elijah and I were best friends."

Best friends until Cal made the choice to step back in a move so final, he rarely returned to Yukon Valley. He used every excuse possible—college, medical school, residency, work. Somewhere along the way, those too-busy excuses turned into his too-busy reality.

He had stayed away for eighteen years.

The only time he had seen Deirdre since high school graduation was at Elijah's bedside when his best friend had a matter of weeks to live. Even then, Cal hadn't been able to speak the words and share with Elijah his regret at stepping aside and effectively cutting Elijah and Deirdre out of his life. No, Cal had cut himself out of *their* lives, and to a large extent the lives of his parents and Yukon Valley.

But at that time, he couldn't do it. To confess, even at Elijah's bedside, felt like betrayal. Still, Cal had made peace with his friend's death shortly after his visit.

Had he made peace with himself? He wasn't willing to explore that question.

However, dropping the death of a friend was one surefire way to shut down people prying in his life. A cop-out, but Cal didn't have the patience to deal with coworkers who, though they might have his best interests at heart, also had way too much free time.

Amberlyn made the face and gave the quick nod people did when they wanted to convey polite but uncomfortable sympathy. "Oh, I-I didn't realize that. I'm sorry for your loss, as well."

Cal made the face and gave the quick nod people did when they needed to make polite but uncomfortable conversation about receiving sympathy. "Thank you." One more grave nod for good measure. "Say, I'm gonna go change, given that I'm coated in black coffee. Be back out in a few minutes."

Cal glanced around the quiet ED. *Quiet* was verboten to speak for anyone who worked in healthcare, regardless of the size or resources of the facility.

Yukon Valley Hospital's trauma level four designated emergency department was a far cry from the level one, busy downtown Seattle ED he staffed. There were five total exam rooms, two of which were generously designated as trauma bays. The trauma designation made him laugh, only because the visiting surgeon came here two days every few weeks on an outreach rotation from Fairbanks. If only the traumas occurred on those exact days during working hours. Never at night or on weekends. Then they'd be set.

His usual workplace, a forty-seven bed ED in the sprawling Harborview Medical Center, received traumas and emergencies from Seattle and surrounding areas. His facility also took patients from local and regional facilities that did not have the resources to manage complex cases. Most days were a nonstop blend of intensity, excitement, and sheer terror, keeping Cal and his colleagues on their toes.

In Yukon Valley, his biggest trauma thus far included himself and coffee. From what he'd gleaned from staff, there were fewer moose accidents than he had envisioned. Regardless of what he was accustomed to, Cal couldn't take a break from work while he spent the next few months helping his parents.

Student loans didn't pay off themselves.

Cal had a job to do here. He also needed to fulfill his obligation as an only son and help Mom at the homestead and Pop through his cardiac recovery.

He glanced around the five pristine and unfortunately empty rooms in the department. Then he spied the two on-shift nurses, quietly talking. Probably plotting.

Yes, a little more ED business would be helpful. Anything to keep the staff too busy for matchmaking.

Stepping into the on-call room, he selected a fresh set of scrubs from the closet and placed the coffee-stained vest at the bottom of his locker.

He stopped and rubbed his palms together, trying to replicate the sensation of having Deirdre in his arms. After all these years.

He dropped a fist onto the locker, enough for the smack of pain to jolt him back to reality.

Unfortunately, his brain wouldn't stop. Not after getting a hint of what he had walked away from years ago.

The definition of torture was the image of Elijah and Deirdre as partners. Happy. Together. Close. He couldn't turn off the mental video. Deirdre had looked up at him mere minutes ago with that gentle smile that hid years of sadness.

Sadness that he wanted to—

To what? What would he do? They had no future.

The first virtual bucket of ice water hit him.

No future.

Then the second virtual bucket woke him the hell up. His chest clenched at the specter of Elijah, his friend's grinning expression warm and welcoming. Cal couldn't compete—wouldn't compete—when it came to his friend.

Resting his head against the cool metal locker door, Cal remembered what it was to be second best.

Why he *was* second best.

Chapter Three

"HEY, SIS, HOW'S it going?"

Deirdre looked up from her office desk. Her younger—but not smaller—brother had arrived early for the Thursday morning seven a.m. district trauma committee meeting. "Busy. The usual. How are the babies doing?"

Mav rolled his eyes as he shrugged out of his labeled navy EMS jacket. "Eating me out of house and home as usual." He loved those motley sled dogs.

Deirdre did too, though nowadays, she never seemed to have time to take them out for a run.

He continued. "Before you ask, I'm fine to handle this weekend's guest arrival. There is only one couple coming in, and I don't have any EMS shifts." His mouth twisted in a rueful expression. "Not sure what outdoor activities the visitors will want to do. Snow's melting, mud's growing. Hope they don't mind getting a little messy."

Deirdre nodded as she shoved her heavy-duty XTRA-TUF boots under her desk. She'd clean the silty wet clumps on the floor before the environmental services staff gave her the stink eye. Ugh. Mud season. Almost as fun as mosquito season, which followed a few months later.

Pivoting in the chair, she slipped on leather pumps appropriate for work. As she stood, Deirdre snagged the black cardigan on the back of her office chair and shrugged it over her beige button-down shirt, all while she glared at her brother.

Going from practical outdoor gear to professional was magical transformation at its finest. "I wasn't going to grill you about your preparations, Mav. I know you have it handled."

"Hey, just covering my bases with a micromanaging older sister. Anticipating fifty questions and all."

"I'm not that bad. Or that much older." She sputtered. "I want to help out with the lodge, though. Do my part in the business."

"As long as you can pinch hit when I'm unavailable, come visit the babies from time to time, and help cover the costs of various repairs and improvements, then that's enough."

She frowned at the clods of mud her brother was shedding from his black EMS work boots as they exited her office. "With Tuli's social media boost, bookings are up. It's nice to see the lodge business moving in the right financial direction for a change."

"Not like it could have gone much further in the other direction. It's a relief, though. Mom and Dad would be proud of us." He rubbed his chin, a mischievous glint in his eye. "Speaking of making Mom and Dad proud …"

Oh, no. Not Mav. She opened her mouth to veer the conversation in a safer direction, but she wasn't fast enough.

"I heard you saw Dr. Garrett."

"Calvin? Sure. We ran into each other."

"Literally, huh."

Billy. She shook an imaginary fist at the sky. If only that busybody would use his powers for good instead of evil.

Straightening, she laughed the story off like it was no big deal. "Nothing like spilling an entire cup of hot coffee on another person to remind us why we're friends. Just like old times."

"Friends?" *Poke.* "Old times?" *Poke, poke.*

Mav might be thirty-four—only two years younger than her—but he was a master of pushing her buttons. Deirdre stiffened her spine. She was having none of the teasing by her younger brother.

Stopping dead in her tracks in the empty admin hallway, she crossed her arms. "Friends." She pinned Mav with what she hoped was her scariest human-resources-about-to-make-a-performance-improvement-plan expression.

"Well, there are worse things to be," he mumbled.

She didn't believe his mildly chastened act for a minute. "Come on now, don't dig for gold that isn't there. I don't have time for this. Don't you have enough going on with your own social life to occupy you?"

"Speaking of digging for gold, no word from that asshole speculator from a month back?"

"Good riddance," she said. "Oh, hey, did you receive the USGS survey paperwork for us to file?"

He nodded. "Should be here today or tomorrow. I'm not letting anyone else take another swing at our land ever again." He faced her with a gleam in his eyes and patted his chest. "Did you like how I changed subjects? You thought I was distracted by a new topic, and you were off the hook. Wrong. Now I'm back."

Damn.

He continued, "Here's the deal. If I can find time in my busy schedule to court Lee, then you could find time to get out there socially as well."

"First of all, I'm an administrator here at the hospital. It's important that I remain professional."

"Sis, I'm dating Dr. Tipton, and we keep things strictly professional in the workplace." He grinned from ear to ear. "And strictly *un*professional outside of the workplace."

Deirdre clapped her hands over her ears. "No. Please, no. I don't want to know the details of my brother's personal life. Dammit to hell, I'm going to have to bleach my eardrums if you keep talking."

He lifted his chin, as if tempting her with a target. "All I'm saying is, it's healthy to date. It's not hard to date. It's not wrong to date. Dating might be good for you." Waving the arm that wasn't holding his jacket, he motioned around them. "Yes, we are in the middle of nowhere. Yes, it's a small community. But people understand that work and personal lives can overlap. Even the lives of, say, a hospital administrator and an ED doc."

Meeting and dating someone, she could tolerate that— even with the small-town microscope.

But the worst-case scenario? Breaking up? Deirdre didn't have enough of a stiff upper lip to face the town's dissection of the emotional fallout. Too many times in her painful past, she had suppressed raw emotions while presenting the veneer of *nothing to see here*. No way would she risk that pain of public assessment again.

"Mav, you've made a lot of assumptions." Walking slowly toward the meeting room with him keeping pace, she said, "Listen, Calvin walked away from Yukon Valley and from Elijah's and my friendship years ago. The only time he came back was when Elijah's impending death forced him to return. Now he's here because of his parents, then he's gone again."

Mav bumped her shoulder with his. "In the meantime, you could still have fun, right?"

First of all, the thought of having *that* sort of fun again? The idea hit her like a kick to the gut. Her husband had died five years ago, and he'd been ill for a year before that. Basic math demonstrated that it had been a long time since she had had *that* kind of fun.

Taking matters into her own hands, so to speak, worked, but it only got a gal so far.

She and Calvin having fun? She gulped and tried to ignore a hot zing of excitement that arrowed straight down to her … fun … center.

Nope. Not having this conversation right now. Not thinking those thoughts right now.

Deirdre spun and stretched to as close to her five-foot, six-inch frame as she possibly could, wishing that her laser glare could burn the smirk off of Mav's face. "You seem like a busy guy, what with being EMS director and running a tourist business. Not much time for anything else."

"Um." His light brown eyebrows drew together.

"So why don't you focus on Mav's life, and I'll work on Deirdre's life. Got it?"

"But—"

"Got. It." She maintained eye contact as she put her hand on the door handle.

He dropped his shoulders, defeated. "Sis, you're kind of scary. You know that, right?"

Deirdre growled at him, opened the door, and flounced into the meeting room. She stumbled mid-flounce, rocking back on her heels.

Calvin sat on the other side of the rectangular table in his ubiquitous scrubs and what appeared to be the freshly washed Patagonia vest. He shuffled the pages of the meeting minutes on the wood laminate tabletop and shot her a brief smile that froze as her leftover glare at Mav caused collateral damage to all in attendance.

Deirdre sucked in a deep breath and pasted what she hoped was a neutral, pleasant, and professional expression on her face. She pulled out a chair, planted her feet flat on the floor, and consciously unclenched her hands, resting them on the boardroom table. There, all better.

Mav took a seat at the head of the table and winked at Deirdre, triggering another prickle of irritation down her spine.

If fratricide wasn't a crime, Deirdre would have committed it multiple times over by now.

"Not enough coffee this morning," she mumbled. Someone snorted. Probably Mav. "Let's get started on our agenda." She shook off the equilibrium-shifting surprise of Calvin's presence.

Of course he was here. Given that he was the only emergency medicine physician on staff, albeit temporarily, he would have been asked to participate on the trauma committee. His insight and experience could be valuable to the group's work of continuously improving the emergency health needs of the community.

Deirdre asked each person to introduce themselves. The emergency department nurse manager, the CEO, and the chief of staff Dr. Burmeister, all greeted Calvin.

Tulimak Sampson, fire chief for the Yukon Valley service district and part-time deli employee at Three Bears, rolled through the door not missing a beat. He greeted everyone as he sat down and introduced himself to Calvin. "Nice to see you again, Doc."

"Again?" Calvin said.

"You were a big shot high school senior when I was in third grade. Surprised you don't remember me. I was scrawny and pestered *everyone*." Tuli paused while several chuckles died down. "Any objection to being part of my various social media campaigns? I know, I know." He waved toward the group, pursed his lips, and intoned, "Not in the hospital unless authorized by the public relations department." He closed one eye and looked at the ceiling. "Do we have one of those departments?"

"I think Deirdre *is* that department," Calvin deadpanned.

Tuli made a face. "Uh-oh."

Calvin pulled his head back. "What's this about the social media campaigns?"

Mav gestured. "Tuli here is single-handedly putting Yukon Valley on the map and boosting tourism. He's doing it by going viral."

"Viral? Hopefully, it's not contagious," Calvin said with a half-smile that made Deirdre's heart stutter.

"Only in a wholesome way." Tuli took his phone and buffed it on his fire department uniform dark button-down shirt before stowing it in his chest pocket. "I'm not aware of any public health risk from my Instagram account." He shot a sideways look at Deirdre. "No patient information is ever shared in anything I do."

"I don't understand the social media angle," Calvin said.

Deirdre pointed to Tuli. "This guy leveraged every single follower on his social media accounts to save our family's lodge."

"Wow," Calvin replied. "That's impressive. How's that involve the hospital?"

"We're in need of more medical staff, and Tuli has the attention of thousands of adventurous social media fans, some of whom work in healthcare." Anna Smits, the fifty-something CEO, steepled her fingers and shot the team an avid and calculating expression that was best labeled Strategic Recruitment Planning.

Tuli puffed out his chest. "It's all in a day's work." He paused. "Hey, Mav, when am I getting a kickback for my efforts with the lodge? I should charge for my influencer services."

"Anyway." Deirdre shook her head as everyone laughed. "Now it's *really* time for us to start our meeting." Papers rustled and pens clicked as the group dove into the agenda items.

What should've been a boring meeting about statistics, case types, utilization trends, and budget was made more interesting by Calvin's presence. He was the only emergency medicine specialized physician that currently worked at this hospital. The family physicians, including chief of staff Dr. Paul Burmeister, normally covered the ED when they were on call for the hospital. Given that they sometimes had to juggle laboring patients, clinic hours, and hospital admissions with stepping away to care for ED patients, the family docs were only too happy to have extra ED support for the next few months.

Deirdre studied the puffy bags under Dr. Burmeister's eyes. Everyone worked way too hard at this hospital. All of the physicians and the staff oftentimes pushed their limits in terms of fatigue and skill. The hospital could hire several more physicians yet still keep everyone busy.

As the local EMS director, Mav finished out the meeting with his report. One ambulance needed repairs. EMS was also looking for more staff to fill shifts so that the current complement of medics didn't have to work overtime. Or worse, to keep shifts from going uncovered.

What surprised her in the report was Mav's mention that he might step back from EMS duties if the lodge's business continued to grow. She hadn't realized that he was thinking about it.

Good for him. Like Deirdre, Mav had buried himself in work when their parents had died. It was easier than dealing with grief. She knew how avoidance worked. After his efforts over the past few years, he had the local EMS service running smoothly and now the family lodge business was coming along.

What went unspoken was the *other* reason he wanted more personal time.

Deirdre was secretly jealous that her brother felt confident enough to set work boundaries and prioritize his personal life and his girlfriend, Lee. Deirdre glanced at Calvin across the table, and he gave her a quick wink. Heat flooded her chest.

If Deirdre truly had an exciting and meaningful personal life, or a family, or hobbies, would she throw herself into her job as much as she did right now? Maybe not, especially if that personal life occurred with one particular person. Her mouth went dry. Moot point.

This was her job. These people were her colleagues. She would continue giving 110 percent and also remain professional, regardless of how much of a tempting vision of a rich life that her brother's example painted. Regardless of ... any other potential temptations.

The meeting shifted to the Breakup Festival and staffing the hospice dunking booth. Anna asked for volunteers, but Deirdre kept quiet and rubbed her sweaty palms on her pants. Her pulse pounded in her head.

Water, ice breaking. Falling into the frigid water, even for a good cause and even with safety measures in place, was a no-go. A cold shiver worked its way into her bones. She couldn't breathe. Her ears buzzed.

Breathe. Push it back. Breathe.

That damned cold wave of grief drowned her at the worst possible times.

Once she had a grip on her emotions, she glanced at Mav. He clearly had guessed why she had clammed up.

"They're still having the Breakup Festival?" Calvin's calm, mellow voice unfroze her.

She sat up straight and met his eyes, his expression thoughtful as he studied her, as if she needed a lifeline to draw her out of her watery grief.

Tuli piped up, "Yeah, and if you are quick about it, you can still place your bid for the exact time the ice breaks."

The absolute last thing Deirdre wanted to do was guess when the damned ice would break.

He continued, "Bidding closes in a few days. The pot is up around fifteen thousand dollars!"

"That's tempting." Calvin gave a deep belly laugh, and Deirdre couldn't help but smile in response. "I do have student loans to pay off."

Anna leaned forward, almost wolverine-like in her focused expression. "I would be remiss in my job duties if I didn't mention that there is a state funded student loan repayment program available for physicians. Every year you practice in an underserved area in Alaska, you get a chunk of your debt subtracted."

Deirdre stared at the paper in front of her like she was cramming for a test. She peeked up at Calvin, who had a thoughtful expression on his face. Calvin here full-time? No way could she avoid him forever.

"Thanks for mentioning it, Anna. I'll keep that in mind, although my plans are to return to Seattle."

"I'm sure Bruce and Aggie would love for you to stick around," Anna said, not giving up. "You'd have a job here."

Deirdre tapped the table with her pen. "Are you ever *not* recruiting, Anna?"

The CEO primly tucked her shoulder-length gray hair back behind an ear. "I take any opportunity that presents itself. You never know when and where you might find great physicians."

Calvin shifted in his seat as silence descended on the room.

"Anyway," Deirdre jumped in, "let's finish with any new agenda items. Our hour is nearly up."

As they finished out the meeting, Calvin met Deirdre's eyes and mouthed, *thank you*.

Chapter Four

L ATER THAT DAY, Cal's ED shift was in full swing.
He'd treated a man with a fracture—the guy's
hammer mistook a finger for a construction nail. The patient
wouldn't be hammering with that hand for a few weeks.

After stabilizing a woman with severe shortness of breath
that turned out to be pneumonia, he placed initial admission
orders. When the patient had come into the ED, her oxygen
levels were in the low eighties. Now, with a dose of steroid
and antibiotics, combined with a breathing treatment and
supplemental oxygen, she breathed much easier. Literally.
Clicking SIGN on the electronic medical record, he sat back
in his chair in the work area. The family physician on call
would finish the orders during rounds later today.

One teen's severe migraine finally responded to a headache cocktail of medications. It was so satisfying to resolve
someone's incapacitating pain and light sensitivity. The big
smile from the grateful patient reminded Cal why he enjoyed
all aspects of ED work, from the straightforward fixes to
those heart-pounding moments when he used his skills to
stabilize traumas and manage acute medical conditions.

The most eye-opening discovery about working in a
smaller facility with lower patient volumes? He had time for

patients and nursing staff. As in, he could actually sit down and talk with them.

Instead of spending the shift calling for stat life-saving equipment and directing personnel through crisis after crisis, he now had the bandwidth to let the patients tell their whole stories. He could truly be present in the exam room instead of always monitoring the unending number of waiting patients in the queue. For the first time in years, he could sincerely ask the *patient what else is concerning you*? and not look at the clock when the patient or family offered more detailed information to help him understand their condition.

His workdays here in Yukon Valley flowed more like a meandering creek than class V rapids, which was different from Harborview's emergency department. He found that he didn't mind the change of pace. *Huh. Go figure.* Cal blinked and rubbed his chin.

His stomach growled. 1:20 p.m. Damn, he'd missed lunch. He hadn't adjusted to the fact that a small hospital cafeteria wasn't open round the clock. He had ninety-minute windows to hit breakfast and lunch.

He'd missed today's window.

Around the corner from his dictation area, the ED doors swung open with a recognizable mechanical clunk and whoosh. For a split second, he tensed, half hoping that a certain person with blue eyes was coming through the doors.

Then he heard a distinctive voice.

"See, I knew he wouldn't stop for lunch." An irritated *hmph.*

Sounded like someone was in trouble, and that someone

was him.

He squirmed in his seat.

"We figured if he didn't need this meal now, he could save it for dinner later."

"That's so sweet of you, Mrs. Garrett." Amberlyn's voice grew louder.

Yep, Mom was here. Cal's actual mother had showed up. In the hospital.

With lunch. For her grown son.

How the mighty had fallen.

"Did you want me to bring some dinner later for you and Clyde, honey?" Aggie said, coming around the corner. "Hi, Calvin!"

"That's nice of you to offer, ma'am." Amberlyn shot an amused expression at Cal. "But we're good."

Pop trudged along behind Mom and squinted around the ED, shaking his head. "Why don't I stay out in the waiting area? Or outside. I don't like keeping Doofus locked in the truck. I hate coming in this place." Good ol' Pop. He had never been jovial, per se, but he'd somehow turned into the town curmudgeon who nowadays seemed to enjoy the company of his mutt more than most people.

"Come this way, Mr. and Mrs. Garrett." Amberlyn directed them to the empty seats on the opposite side of Cal's work area.

Mom said, "We don't want to disturb patients—"

Patients. Mom didn't care about disturbing Cal. He snorted, then froze when Amberlyn glared at him.

"It's no disturbance," she said sweetly. "We're between

patients. There's no problem with you being here right now."

No problem, other than the fact that families did not generally bring lunch *directly into their family member's workplace*. In the hospital. But hello, Yukon Valley.

Clyde, the other nurse on shift, popped his head out from where he was restocking supplies. "Hey, I thought I heard familiar voices!" Strolling over, he rested his clipboard on the fax machine. "Um, Aggie, I don't suppose you brought any of those world-famous chocolate chip cookies?"

"As a matter of fact, I did bring you all a batch." Mom pulled out two old Christmas tins.

The unit coordinator pushed back from her workstation and quickly joined the party.

Mom added, "You have to share these with the rest of the team, Calvin."

The two nurses and the unit coordinator laughed and ribbed Cal. Their laughs turned to happy sighs as they bit into Mom's cookies.

He peeked in the paper bag and inhaled. "Meatball sandwich?"

"One of your favorites," Mom said, smacking Pop's hand as he reached for a cookie. "That's for the ED. Your batch is at home."

"It's not as good. It's my no cholesterol, low sugar batch." Pop groused and waved his hands. "Don't you people do any work around here? Seems like a lot of goofing off happening."

Amberlyn pointed her half-eaten cookie like a weapon,

making Pop's eyes bulge. "Bruce, we love you, but you don't get to complain about how hard we work."

After eating the last of his cookie, Clyde crossed his arms across his chest and stood next to Amberlyn in nursing solidarity.

Mom gave Pop the we're-going-to-talk-about-this-later look.

"Um." Sweat beaded Pop's forehead.

Calvin swallowed a bite, the savory meatball and home-made sourdough bread taking him back to meals from years ago. He laughed but did not put down the sandwich. "Well, Pop, you stepped in it now. Rule one. Never ever insult the nurses. That's biting the hand that feeds you. I believe the last time you saw these *goofing off* folks, you were nearly dead."

Clyde waggled a finger before snagging another cookie. "As I recall, the very last time Bruce was here, he was fine even though he was faking a heart attack as he helped us play matchmaker with Dr. Lee and Maverick Steen. The time before that"—he paused for effect—"Bruce wasn't nearly dead. He was very much dead. We *goof-offs* made him undead. Come to think of it, we should get chocolate chip cookies for the rest of our careers."

Mom nodded, ignoring the dissatisfied man next to her. "I tried to explain this to him, but this fellow ... if you told him the sky was blue, he'd argue that it was red."

"Sometimes it *is* red," Pop grumbled.

Cal chuckled then sobered. Pop *had* died here in the ED. Even after the team obtained return of spontaneous circulation after the massive heart attack, Pop's clinical situation had been dicey for the next forty-eight hours. A heart cath and stents had made a huge difference, but the cardiologists hadn't been able to guarantee that everything would turn out all right. Sure enough, Pop's stay in the ICU in Fairbanks hadn't been uncomplicated, either. He might never regain all of his heart function due to the cardiac damage.

Glaring at Pop, Mom turned back to the staff and said sweetly, "Next time, if you could leave that throat tube in place so he can't talk back, I'll double your future cookie orders."

"Deal," Amberlyn said.

Right as Clyde replied, "Done!"

"You people are ganging up on us old folks." Pop gestured toward himself.

"They're giving you a taste of the grief you give them," Mom said.

"I heard that you like the grief I give you, dear." Pop waggled his bushy eyebrows.

Mom's cheeks turned pink. "Oh, Bruce."

Seriously, this could not be Cal's life right now. He finished off the sandwich and wadded up the wax paper, tossing it into the trashcan. "You two"—he wiped his face with a napkin and threw that in the bin as well—"need to take these shenanigans outside. The hospital is no place for canoodling."

Everyone laughed, including Mom and Pop. It felt good. It felt right. Comfortable.

Amberlyn slung an arm around Mom's shoulders. "Say, don't you think Dr. Garrett would benefit from some canoodling? Maybe with someone working in the hospital?"

Alarm klaxons went off in Cal's brain. *Redirect the conversation. Now!*

Mom laughed and gently bumped Amberlyn's hip with hers. "We've been telling him this for years. We even have suggestions, but he won't listen to us."

Clyde, who was married with two children, nodded sagely like a bald oracle on the relationship mountaintop. "Maybe he needs a good push in the right direction? We can help. We're good at that."

Cal held up his hands like he was holding back a leaking dam. His effort was about as effective. "Okay, folks. No pushes. No direction. Time to finish the cookies and get back to work." He gritted his teeth at the motionless staff who were *not* done with the cookies and who were obviously *not* going back to work. "Hello?"

By now Mom and Pop had huddled with Clyde and Amberlyn about three feet away from Cal.

"Anyone?" It was like talking to a wall. "As the ED doc, aren't you all supposed to listen to me?"

The unit coordinator touched her silver curls and smiled, creasing the lines in her face. "I'm listening." She peeked at the tin. "And I do believe I might have another cookie." She, too, however, did not make a move to return to her desk.

Bruce looked back over his shoulder at Cal. "I mean, if it weren't for me, those other two would never have gotten together. I'm on a roll."

Mom shook her head. "No, dear. Flirting with death isn't the same as helping people flirt."

Amberlyn peered at Clyde and then at Cal's parents. "What we need to do is get him a date for the Breakup Festival."

Cal gave up. Medical hierarchy had deteriorated into straight-up anarchy. He kept his head down, pretended to review lab results, and polished off another delicious cookie. The still-warm chocolate melted in his mouth. Okay, fine. There might be a few advantages to working in the same town as his parents.

People plotting his future relationships? That was where he had to draw the line.

His ears burned, knowing that people were talking about him. "Okay, dream team. If you're not an employee at this facility, then I suggest you head on out because actual employees at this facility have real work to do."

Mom made a *hmph*.

Pop studied him until his back prickled with sweat. Cal wanted to shrug out of his vest. It had suddenly become warm in here.

"Use your energy for hospital things," he said, trying to project authority. He wiped his hands on a napkin then reached for a squirt of foaming hand sanitizer. "No dates for the festival. Besides, my time here in Yukon Valley is temporary until Mom and Pop get more support."

Pop crossed his arms and planted his feet. Uh-oh. "Who needs more support?" Pop asked. "I'm not an invalid. Aggie and I are taking care of the homestead just fine. Besides, we've got all the support we need right from all of our extended *family* here in Yukon Valley."

That word snapped like a rubber band on Cal's wrist. Hard enough to sting and get his attention.

Pop puffed up his chest, winding up even more. "Yukon Valley has everything that I need. It has a hospital, nice people, and folks willing to help at any time."

Amberlyn, Clyde, and the unit secretary all nodded.

"It doesn't have a cardiologist," Cal said.

"The chance of me needing another cardiologist anytime soon is pretty small, now that my heart has been roto-rootered and the pipes reinforced."

Mom shook her head.

Amberlyn and Clyde chuckled and drifted away.

That left Calvin with a potential unpleasant argument brewing with Pop. It was a familiar argument about his parents' future. He was not going to have it here in his place of work.

"Let's talk about this later, Pop. It's not something we need to decide today." Truth be told, Cal had considered all the options and had decided on the best course of action.

If only he could get his parents on the same page. What they needed was a push in the right direction. He glanced at his phone. There had been a text earlier this week that might provide that push. Cal needed to take time to think this plan through.

Pop huffed. "Maybe you won't be in such a rush to get me out of Yukon Valley if you had a good reason to want to stay here."

Chapter Five

O N FRIDAY MORNING, Deirdre greeted the food services staff as she loaded up her morning coffee in the cafeteria, careful not to spill on her cream-colored blouse and khaki pants.

A familiar warm chuckle sent a frisson of excitement down her spine. She immediately squared her shoulders before turning around.

"I see we had the same idea this morning." Calvin lifted his metal tumbler in a greeting.

Damn him, but he looked no worse for wear in his typical scrubs and vest, despite having finished his twenty-four-hour shift. In fact, the light stubble on his chin gave him a rugged appearance that woke her up faster than Yukon Valley hospital's black coffee.

"Did you have a good shift?" she said.

Calvin scrubbed his lightly stubbled face, the rough sound popping on her nerve endings. "The medical part was no problem." He shot her a wry grin.

Her toes curled, and she gripped the coffee carafe.

With a nod, he continued in a low voice, "The sheer amount of meddling in my personal life from Mom and Pop, who are in cahoots with every hospital employee, is exhausting."

Dee paused mid-pour. "Wait. You, too?" She kept her voice low also.

The food services staff were nice, but they heard *everything* in the hospital.

"Damn it. If you're fair game for the Yukon Valley matchmaking team, and you're admin, then I've got no chance."

"Are they being unprofessional?" This was a more casual work environment where most staff members knew each other outside of the hospital. However, if necessary, Deirdre would redirect the staff regarding boundaries and maintaining professionalism in the workplace.

"Mom and Pop? Always unprofessional."

"No, the staff."

"They do a great job, and the camaraderie is excellent. I don't want to mess with their teamwork. But they're applying that teamwork to other areas of my life." He took a sip. "It's more about them having conversations and poking gentle fun. I'm not looking to get anyone in trouble."

Deirdre shook her head. "I thought it was mostly me that the staff had focused on. Mav, too. Seems like ever since he got hooked up, Mav has time to spare to evaluate my nonexistent dating life."

"Not sure about Maverick's motives, but with the staff I'm sure they have good intentions. We're all friends here, so I don't take offense."

"It's not interfering with your work?"

"Nope."

"Do you feel comfortable stopping it if need be?"

"Yep." He flashed a thoughtful expression. "Although, I'd hate to take away all of their fun."

With a laugh that bubbled up from deep inside, she stared at Calvin's familiar but handsome face. Her old friend. *We're all friends here*, he had said. Old friends who could put a plan together like no one's business.

Something resembling an idea started to take shape. Deirdre tapped the mug with a finger.

"Uh-oh. You're plotting." He gently bumped her upper arm with his elbow.

"Just thinking that"—she dumped cream in her coffee and stirred—"your problem sounds exactly like my problem."

"Huh."

"My problem is being the focus of the staff's machinations. Looks like they have similar goals for you."

"It's also uncomfortable for you when they ask kind but probing questions?"

"Yes!" she said too loudly, then quickly smiled at the employee nearby. She sipped the coffee to lower the fluid level in the mug so that any wild gesture of hers was less likely to spill.

Calvin's dark eyebrows shot up. "We have the same problem." He looked around to make sure no eavesdroppers lurked nearby. "Are you thinking what I'm thinking?"

No. No way. She shivered. The plan had risk, but also a chance of relieving the pressure.

It could work. "I think I am. And I believe we should

have a meeting. Right now."

"Where?" He made a face before taking a drink of his coffee.

"My office." She tilted her head toward the staff milling around in the cafeteria. "You'd rather we meet here?"

"No, I do not." He paused and pulled his buzzing phone from the vest pocket. "Pardon me a second." She tried not to peek as Calvin studied the screen, frowned, swiped the screen, and put the phone back in his pocket.

"Everything okay?" she said.

His expression smoothed out in a split second, but his smile was tighter than normal. "Nothing we need to worry about. Let's go." He mirrored her businesslike stride and posture as they collegially walked side-by-side to the administration suite.

Once safely in her office, Calvin shut the door with a gentle, solid sound.

A sound of finality and promise.

She wetted her lips and motioned toward her small round meeting table. Calvin settled in a chair, and Deirdre took the seat next to him and scooted it to face him. "Don't get me wrong. I love the staff. It's very nice that they're trying to help me out. It's nice that they care about others," she began.

"I agree. However, they are wearing me down, and I've only been here for two shifts. There's a lot more scheduled. If I have to answer one more question about when am I settling down and having kids, I might jump out the window."

A snort-laugh erupted, and Deirdre was darn lucky she hadn't been mid-sip of coffee. "This is a one-story building!"

"I didn't say my action would be effective. Mostly demonstrative." Even though Calvin sat casually with an ankle resting on his knee, leaning back in the chair, he somehow managed to take up space and air in the small room. He put the coffee tumbler on the table. "You're suggesting we work together to remove us as targets for the staff's plotting pleasure?"

"Exactly."

"So."

"Um."

"Pretend to be together." His storm-cloud gray gaze pinned her in place.

He had said the words she couldn't.

Her heart kicked an extra beat, and it didn't have to do with the caffeine. Could she do this? Could she survive being closer to Calvin but pretending? For how long? So many details swirled in her mind.

Still, the chance of a reprieve from the kindhearted, relentless prying tempted her.

Calvin planted both feet on the floor and leaned forward. He peered at Deirdre long enough for her to memorize the fine lines bracketing the set of his mouth. "Cards on the table," he said.

Deirdre's cards were way too complicated when it came to Calvin. Her past and their past and her feelings and whatever his feelings were all obscured the water like glacier melt in a slow-moving river. So much existed beneath the surface that she couldn't see.

Wouldn't examine.

Deirdre swallowed again. True, the last several years of grief and immersion into work as her go-to avoidance technique had gotten old. Everyone in town and in the hospital knew her story. Everyone had decided it was time for her to move on with her life.

Except Deirdre.

Her life was a well-oiled machine, efficient and productive. Fulfilling. Her daily job contained enough uncertainty and change. She wasn't prepared to bring that level of uncertainty and change to her personal life.

What she and Calvin proposed might get everyone off her back for a while. Relieve the social pressure.

Tempting.

Almost as tempting as the tall, lean frame of the man she had known for years. Yet, here he sat, so much about him now unfamiliar due to physical distance and the passage of time.

What she did truly know about this present-day Calvin? Not much, except that he was still her friend.

Deirdre's therapist would have a heyday with this elaborate decision to avoid addressing her issues.

Avoidance sounded darn good to Deirdre.

She took a fortifying sip of black gold and mirrored his forward posture, resting one arm on the table next to her. "Okay. I have a few cards I can lay out for you. Here's the deal. I don't have time or energy for a relationship. However, like you said, it's exhausting having everyone poke around in my personal life. Frankly, I can't handle the poking right now. If I hear one more comment about taking a date to the Breakup Festival, I will jump out the window right behind you.

"All of my spare time is taken up by work or helping Mav with the lodge. Or, here recently, defending against those idiots who want to access to claims in this area."

A land speculator, Randy Nelson, had posed as a guest at the lodge over a month ago in early February. He had faked an accident to try to financially ruin Deirdre and Mav so he could purchase the property along with newly discovered valuable mineral rights. They had squashed Randy's threats to their family home and land but were determined to get the property legally squared away so nothing like this could surprise them again.

"I'm too busy for anything actually resembling a real relationship." She wrapped up her rant.

A tiny inkling niggled at her. If she did have a quality partner, she would *make* time. But as of now, that idea continued to be a nonstarter. There was a saying that work expanded to fit the time available, and her life was a prime example. Her life was full of professionally satisfying activities that wouldn't hurt her.

Calvin laced his long, tapered fingers together, making tendons move on the back of his hands and his hair-dusted forearms. "Then we are in complete agreement. I think the only way we can get folks off our backs is to start dating. At least until after the Breakup Festival."

"Break up after the breakup?"

"The irony is not lost on me." His boyish grin caught her off guard for a split second, transporting her back to her senior year in high school when two men held special places in her heart. That was then.

Then didn't matter.

In the present, she and Calvin were two totally different people in a totally different situation with very different needs. "We'll have to continue working together. Can you separate your professional relationship from a pretend relationship?" she asked.

"Pretending is one of my best skills."

She laughed, because any other reaction meant she acknowledged how the truth hit too close to home for her as well. Pretending to be okay. Pretending to have dealt with her grief. Pretending to be part of normal society. "Me, too!"

"Then we might have a deal." Calvin stuck out his hand with a businesslike dip of his chin. "Deirdre Steen, would you agree to pretend to date me?"

Chapter Six

CAL IGNORED THE zip of warmth as Deirdre's soft, warm palm pressed against his. He ignored how perfectly their hands fit together. He ignored the curve of her full breasts under that silky, cream-colored blouse or the cute wiggle in her walk that those slacks showcased perfectly.

Ignored all of it. Because his was a business deal, born out of necessity. He had been driven to this decision by friends and family who had way too much free time. Technically, this farce was all their fault.

Technically, he and Deirdre weren't really dating.

Technically, he had no feelings for Deirdre.

Damn it.

In medicine, he had learned early on to respect his patients when they described a sense of impending doom.

He had that same sense right now, settling heavy on his shoulders. Had he permanently altered a friendship of so many years, all for a self-serving lie?

If that was the case, so be it. This was a mutual decision with mutual benefit. Hey, Cal lived to be helpful to others.

He completed the handshake and eased back in the seat.

"So, how are we going to go about this ... thing?" she said, her gaze sliding past his right ear to somewhere behind him.

Inappropriate answers, each one more sensual than the last, fast-forwarded through his mind.

Somehow, he focused and choked out, "An agreement. An informal verbal contract."

Deirdre bit her lower lip, burning the image into his brain. A bolt of desire shot through him, and he shifted in his seat to manage his quickly changing anatomy.

"Go on," she said, cheeks pink.

"We need terms. Rules."

"You want me to get a pad and paper? We might need a notary public." She took a few steps to her desk, returning with writing materials.

Cal laughed. "I think our handshake deal is solid."

"I don't know. How binding is this agreement? Do we need witnesses? I mean, you seem trustworthy enough." She tilted her head and pushed her short hair behind both ears with a mischievous expression.

His abdomen tightened. He wanted to touch her pink cheeks and see if they were as warm as they appeared.

He curled his hand into a light fist. "Absolutely trustworthy. You can check my doctor ratings at RateYourDoc.com to verify. I also have references upon request. No malpractice claims either, knock on wood."

"That's medicine. This is dating. Maybe I *should* contact references?"

"In full disclosure, I don't have a real extensive history on the résumé when it comes to dating." He wasn't embarrassed to admit it. Busy schedules made for limited relationships.

Guilt about his best friend and years of conflicted feelings about his high school crush didn't help his dating activity. No partner had ever come close to Deirdre-level quality. At least, not the ideal version of Deirdre he'd created in his mind years ago. He had added layers to the iconic image as memories blurred. The person he envisioned now was darn near untouchable in a competition with any other woman.

Deirdre tapped the pen, making small blue marks on the pad. She didn't meet his eyes. "Are you sure you want to do this?"

"We're making an informed decision, weighing out the risks versus benefits." He took a fortifying sip of coffee. "I sure as heck don't want to play twenty uncomfortable questions about how I should be seeing someone. Not on every shift, and not with my parents."

"I understand completely." She heaved in a big breath and rolled her lips. "Then let's do this. Ground rules? Terms?"

Rubbing his chin with his index finger, he said, "First of all, we have to sell the scenario. We're already under a microscope. If there's any doubt in our sincerity, then the social examination is going to get worse, not better. I don't want to give Mom and Pop too much to chew on."

"What do you mean by *sell*?" she asked.

His gaze studied her slender neck as she swallowed. Was she affected by him like he was by her? No way.

"We should incorporate the Breakup Festival into our plans," he said.

"Agreed. That will calm the rabid hordes of matchmakers. How about … going out one day per week and attending the Breakup Festival together."

"That feels too light," he said. He wanted to spend more time with her. This contract gave him a great excuse. "No one's going to buy it. Not around here. They're like starving dogs spotting a bone." He smiled at her involuntary snort. If only he could bottle that happiness and sell it. Or save it for future times when he needed it. "We have to go all-in." He looked up at the tiled ceiling, then back to Deirdre.

Her chest rose and fell. "What do you think it will take?"

No way was he touching the real answer trying to claw its way out of his chest. "How about two casual but intentionally public dates-slash-outings each week and then attending the Breakup Festival and dance together?" He expected to be heading back to Seattle shortly after the festival, so the timing would work.

"I could fit that into my calendar. How about you?" she asked with a tentative but game grin.

How the hell am I having this conversation? The stagecoach horses are stampeding away without anyone at the reins.

Calvin wiped a sweaty palm on his scrub pants. "Yes. I will manage two dates per week until the Breakup Festival."

She laughed out loud again. "I mean, if it's going to be a hardship …"

The hardship wouldn't be the dating part. Not with Deirdre.

It would be the not-dating part.

He considered his coffee, wishing it contained something

to better fortify his courage. "Let me do a teach-back communication technique."

"Again with the learning modules. Seriously?" Deirdre waved her fingers. "Fine. Go on with demonstrating your patient communication skills, which in turn will increase your Press-Ganey scores."

"My Press-Ganey scores reflect on the institutions that I serve. It is in everyone's best interest for those scores to be high."

"I don't know how you can keep a straight face, but I'm all ears."

He pressed his hand against the table. "Ahem. Here's what I am hearing from our conversation. Please let me know if I have misunderstood anything."

Her brows rose. "You bet I will."

He held up index and middle fingers. "We have agreed to have two dates per week"—then the thumb of the other hand—"for one month. Then a grand finale date at the Breakup Festival."

"Financial considerations?"

"I'll pay for the dates."

"But—"

"We have to make it look good. People will talk if we split costs."

"I can pay you back."

"I'm pretty sure my credit card can handle the burden of an extra mouth to feed."

"Now I'm a burden?" Even as she narrowed her gaze, her blue eyes twinkled.

The words left him before he could stop them. "You are anything but a burden."

Uncomfortable silence was punctuated by an overhead page for environmental services to the med-surg unit. He and Deirdre waited until the page repeated three times, per hospital protocol.

His heart thundered against his ribs. "Let's talk about actionable items."

"Sorry?" Something in that wide-eyed expression ... he couldn't stop staring.

"We need to act like we're dating."

"Not while we're working," she interjected.

"We can be casual and friendly at work. Appropriate. Nothing overt. But we can make it look good in other venues. How about PG-rated PDA during those two dates a week?"

"Define PG-rated."

For a solid ten seconds, he could only come up with R-rated or higher examples that made him want to lick and nibble her neck and lips. He wanted to kiss and paw at her like the voracious non-boyfriend he was.

He shook his head, trying to loosen those ideas. "We will proceed as though we've never dated anyone before, ever. Start with gazes, handholding, and hugs. We can consider a public kiss in the moment, if we agree on it and if we need a witness."

"For the sake of pretense."

"Of course."

"I can get on board with that."

Cal couldn't. Proximity to Deirdre was dangerous. Period.

She leaned forward, providing a hint of shadow between her breasts that tempted him to imagine more. "Topics of dating conversation?" she asked. "Are there any relationship progress benchmarks we need to achieve? Metrics?"

"You're such an administrator. Next you'll want me to use evidence-based communication in fake-dating." He went still and stared at her.

Deirdre's eyes glinted. "Don't worry. We won't use AIDET customer service training in our dating life!"

"Really? Could be fun." He leaned back and crossed his arms over his chest, deep in contemplation. "All right. Appearances count more than anything. Given that we're not in this for the long haul, I vote no deep topics. No probing questions."

"Light and breezy sounds great to me!"

"Then we break up after the festival with no hard feelings, and I return to my regular life in Seattle. You go on about your business, secure in the fact that you both satisfied and thwarted the devious local matchmakers." His stomach clenched.

The frown and droop to her lips lasted a split second.

This was what they both wanted. Wasn't it?

"Works for me." It was impressive how Deirdre had mastered the art of remaining objective and neutral.

Cal hoped he also had that skill right about now. "Do we shake on it or … hug on it?" He stood up when she did.

Deirdre seemed to freeze for a moment, her hands gripping the edge of the table. After a pause, she said, "Well, we have to start somewhere."

"How about we practice the PG-rated PDA?" Cal extended his arms to the side.

Deirdre took a few steps to meet him, sliding her arms around him with such a light touch, that at first, he questioned whether she even made contact. He put his arms around her. Tender. Friendly. His heartrate spiked. The gentle press of her frame that tucked perfectly against his shifted something in his brain. They fit too well.

He inhaled deeply her light floral and crisp linen scent. Some things never changed.

Every muscle in his body relaxed. Her presence did that to him.

Damn it, this could turn out to be a terrible decision.

Chapter Seven

THE NEXT MONDAY afternoon, Deirdre dragged herself through work. She trudged down the hall from labor and delivery past med-surg and headed toward the ED, cafeteria, and then admin. Even her bones ached. Too many meetings today, too many emails.

Too much work at the lodge this past weekend. Mav's plan to host the guests had imploded when one of the EMTs called out sick. Exit Mav.

Enter Deirdre. While Mav pulled an impromptu twenty-four-hour shift, she had cleaned the lodge, fixed breakfast for the couple, knocked a few repairs off the lodge business's to-do list, and took the sled dogs out for two slushy, yappy trots.

All of that extra work meant Deirdre had to bail on Saturday's first fake-date with Calvin. Rescheduling to Sunday was a bust as well, as she had to pinch hit in med-surg for the Sunday night shift when two nurses called out sick.

Deirdre took pride in the care this critical access hospital provided, but having a small but dedicated staff meant that the healthcare delivery system strained under the weight of even one unanticipated absence. At the end of the day, patient safety came first. What Deirdre wished was to snap her fingers and *poof*, there would appear a bunch of extra nurses and nursing assistants. Harsh reality meant that regardless of ongoing recruiting efforts and generous incentives, rural areas everywhere had a steep hill to climb to find enough staff.

This Monday hit harder than usual, what with her job, the lodge, and sorting out the mineral rights for the property so Randy couldn't try again to access their land. She and Mav had more paperwork to review and an upcoming meeting with an attorney.

Somewhere in all of these activities, she needed to pretend to date Calvin while trying to avoid feelings and not dealing with her past. Everything dragged at her like a lead radiology apron on weary shoulders.

There wasn't enough caffeine to get through this day. Here she was at three o'clock, heading to the cafeteria to consider another cup. She tugged on the sleeves of her gray blazer and smoothed the matching gray pants and rosé wine-colored shirt, hoping she still appeared professional instead of flat-out haggard.

Last weekend illustrated exactly why she hadn't entertained the idea of a real relationship. See? She couldn't even get a fake relationship off the ground.

But she didn't want it to get off the ground.

Damn it all, a small part of her had looked forward to dinner with Calvin.

Deirdre peered out the glass wall in the main entrance. A snow squall swirled, the pine and scrub-filled hills in the distance no longer visible. Typical for late March in Alaska's interior. One minute sun and the next minute a whiteout. She had worn her mud boots to work, not her snow boots. Either would get her home well enough, but it was hard to plan attire for every weather possibility.

"Trauma alert, ED. Trauma alert, ED. Trauma alert, ED." The voice blaring over the intercom startled her.

Deirdre spun and hurried to the ED. She wasn't required to attend trauma alerts or codes, but oftentimes these events could use an extra set of hands.

Arriving in the emergency department, she skidded to a halt.

The raised voices in trauma room one didn't catch her attention. The Velcro rip of a blood pressure cuff, an unidentified metal clank, and rumbling wheels of rolling equipment didn't, either.

But the trail of thick, bloody gurney tracks on the floor leading from the EMS entrance into the trauma bay triggered a mental switch that took her from surprised to laser-focused in a split second.

She snagged a pair of gloves from the box hanging on the wall outside the trauma room, stepped over a fresh red puddle on the floor, and stopped short. Mav and Louise had just finished offloading their patient. Both the seasoned EMTs expressions were lip-tightened and grim.

Nurses Amberlyn and Clyde both had their jaws dropped, even as they scrambled to hook up leads and obtain vitals.

Deirdre's neck prickled.

Leaning over the patient—or rather climbing on top

of—was Calvin, his bloody, gloved hands pressed against the upper thigh of the patient. Deirdre peeked and gasped.

"Hi, Deirdre," the patient said with a weak wave.

Tuli?

What the hell had happened?

Good God, blood was everywhere.

When Mav loosened the field tourniquet and Calvin moved his hand for a moment, a bright red spray fountained straight up from Tuli's bare thigh and splattered his thermal shirt and what remained of his thin snow pants and thermal base layer. As someone who hailed from the local Athabascan native population, Tuli's complexion normally had a warm tone.

Right about now, he was whiter than the one small remaining unstained portion of the hospital sheet beneath him.

Calvin caught Deirdre's eye. His intense, almost blank stare with the raised brows made her knees knock together. It took a lot to rattle the EMTs and the nurses. It took far more than that to rattle a doc from a Seattle tertiary center's ED. He'd seen it all.

This situation was bad. Very bad.

"What the heck happened?" she said.

Mav shrugged. "Leave it to Tuli, but he decided to snowmachine his body directly into a broken tree branch."

"What?"

Tuli shook his head. "That's what I said. The trail was clear a few days ago. I was helping out Uncle Leonard by checking traps before the storm, figured I'd speed things up by using the snowmachine. Still not sure how it happened. It was like a bunch of branches had been shaved and set up to face the trail. I had stood up to see over a rise. One of the branches caught me. It was sharp enough to come through my clothes. Probably due to speed. Though I wasn't speeding! Force plus velocity plus sharp pointy object equals…" He took a shaky breath. "Oh, man. It could have been someone else on that trail. A different injury. Worse."

Deirdre glanced at Mav, who frowned. She knew that look. He'd make sure law enforcement checked out the accident site after things stabilized here.

She jumped in. "What can I do to help?"

Calvin paused and stared at Tuli, then met her eyes. "He needs emergency surgery."

She squinted at the ceiling. Monday. "We don't have our outreach surgeon here today. The CRNA is likely breaking away from an endoscopy case to get over here as soon as possible." She turned to the unit coordinator to confirm. "OR crew should be in-house for the endoscopy cases, so they can prep an OR."

The coordinator continued to scribe the trauma timeline while dialing her portable phone.

"An OR for whom?" He grimaced, his gray eyes wry and intense. "None of those things are a surgeon, just surgeon-adjacent."

"Transfer?" she asked Calvin. Asked the room. Anyone.

Mav piped up from outside the room where he'd parked his gurney, "We could go by ground, but I don't think that's wise. Latest weather update says that this storm is set to turn into a blizzard here in the next hour." He glanced over at

Louise, who nodded as she wiped down the bloody EMS gurney. "Skies might clear tomorrow for Fairbanks to fly a fixed wing to our local airfield, but not anytime soon. No chopper today with the wind and snow, obviously."

"Damn it." Calvin's chest rose and fell, slowly. It was a deliberate movement. His voice came out tight, controlled. "Okay. So, we have no transfer ability and no surgeon, but we need both right now."

Tuli's head rolled weakly from side to side, but he gave a small laugh. "Yo, people, I might not be a fancy doctor, but I am a first responder. I know what a punctured femoral artery acts like." His voice shook. "Gotta say, the irony is not lost on me. I did not plan to go out in this kind of blaze of glory." He glanced toward the glass door where Louise grimly continued to clean equipment.

Amberlyn placed a second large-bore IV and hooked up another bolus liter of IV fluid. "I'm surprised you aren't livestreaming this on your socials, Tuli."

"I asked Lou in the ambulance, but she wouldn't let me," he whined. "We'd be going viral by now." He flashed a halfhearted smile, goofy if not for the white-rimmed fear in his eyes. "I like to say that I'll do anything for likes and follows, but this isn't what I meant." He paused. "It was kind of weird getting a callout for myself after my cousin called 911. Glad he was riding in the machine behind me, not in front of me."

Louise scowled at him as she shrugged out of her blood-soaked EMS jacket and cleaned her blood-spattered face with the skin-safe sanitizing wipes Mav offered her. Neither

Louise nor Mav went far. As Yukon Valley district fire chief, Tuli was part of the local first responder team. He was one of their own. One of the community's own. If he'd been any farther away when the accident occurred, he wouldn't be alive right now.

Deirdre's heart thudded double-time.

Calvin looked down at where his hand pressed against the upper leg, then said, "Let's get two units of blood, stat. How fast can we have a crossmatch?"

The lab tech waiting at the doorway said, "As soon you give me the tubes, I should have crossmatched blood ready in fifteen minutes."

"Let's do that," Calvin said.

Deirdre could only guess at what it took for him to remain this composed.

Amberlyn handed off the requested blood specimen from the rainbow set of vials she had drawn.

Calvin called to the retreating lab tech, "Also send over two units of O negative blood to have at bedside, stat. In case it takes longer than fifteen minutes for crossmatch or we need blood sooner." He took in another huge breath, his shoulders heaving up and down, like a methodical, centering movement. "What are the latest vitals?"

"Blood pressure one-oh-eight over sixty. Pulse one ten. Oxygen sat ninety-six percent," Amberlyn responded.

Calvin nodded and glanced at the ceiling. "Someone get, ah, Fairbanks acute care surgery on-call on the phone." He lifted his hand, and another gush of blood poured out. "Shit. Maverick, tighten that tourniquet again. Looks like I'm going to need a lot of exposure, good lighting, and an extra set of hands." His grim gaze locked onto Deirdre's with what felt like an iron *clink* of resolute determination.

She swallowed. She had some experience many years ago as an OR nurse. Time to dust off those rusty skills. She shrugged out of her jacket, which she placed on the counter. She took the laceration repair tray Clyde had retrieved, opened it in sterile fashion, placed it on the metal Mayo stand, and waited for Calvin's next request.

"Which docs are here today?" she asked, eyeing her brother as he retightened the field tourniquet on the upper thigh until Tuli grimaced.

The unit coordinator pulled up information on her tablet. "Dr. Burmeister is doing the case in endoscopy right now. Nurse practitioner in the clinic. Dr. Tipton is in labor and delivery with a patient who is pushing."

"So, you're saying there's lots of help, just not for me." His mirthless laugh sent a chill down Deirdre's spine. "We can't wait for one of them." Calvin turned to Tuli. "We're going to take care of you." As Mav increased the tourniquet tightness, Calvin released the downward pressure from his hands and grunted in what sounded like temporary satisfaction.

"I trust you, Doc," Tuli's voice had grown weaker. "You got this."

"Pull up twenty ccs of lidocaine for local injection," Calvin said to Clyde.

"Wait, what?" Tuli squawked. "My *atta boy* didn't mean you could try to repair my femoral artery while I'm awake."

He eyed the large syringe. "Are you kidding me?"

"If our CRNA rolls in here soon, you can take a nap."

"Sure, tempt me with the good drugs." Tuli's speech slurred. "Hoo, boy. I don't feel so good." His eyes rolled back, and his head lolled to one side. Out.

"Repeat vitals now," Calvin said, so calmly. Too calm. He glanced over to the unit coordinator. "Do we have Fairbanks yet?"

The woman held out the phone. "I've got Dr. Yang on the line. She's on call for trauma surgery."

"Put her on speaker." Calvin projected his voice toward the phone that the coordinator placed in the nearby vitals machine basket. "Hey, this is Cal Garrett, ED doc out here in Yukon Valley. We've got a femoral artery puncture, snowmachine rider versus sharp object. Unstable vitals. No surgeon and no ability to transfer for at least twenty-four hours. This facility doesn't have enough blood products to stay ahead of the hemorrhaging."

"Sounds like you need to do a femoral artery repair."

"That's where you come in," Calvin said.

After one crisp chuckle, Dr. Yang got down to business. "With the right tools, you can fix most anything anywhere. It might be a little messy." She paused. "You're going to do great. Can we establish a proper telehealth link so I can see what you're doing?"

The coordinator and Clyde rolled in the telehealth video console and set up the connection.

Sweat rolled down Deirdre's back. This room was getting more crowded by the minute.

Calvin tilted his chin. "Thanks, Dr. Yang. This isn't a situation I personally encountered at Harborview, due to having ample operating room availability and acute care surgeons always in-house."

The trauma surgeon adjusted the camera remotely, so it angled toward Tuli. She peered at her screen. "This is par for the course for remote Alaska sites. I walked a family doctor through an appendectomy in Kotzebue a while back. Yours will not be the first assist I've performed from hundreds of miles away."

"Glad you're confident." Calvin grimaced. "Deirdre, can you help?"

"Yes." If he was going to attempt to save Tuli's life and limb, then she would do her best to assist him. Her mouth dry, she gulped, donned a mask and eye shields, then shrugged into a sterile gown, cuffing on fresh gloves.

With the tourniquet in place, the bleeding from the open puncture wound had slowed to a trickle.

Tuli's right leg blanched.

Minimal blood flow to the limb. How long could that go on without causing damage? She didn't know.

The CRNA, Tom, arrived out of breath and already banging open drawers on the ED anesthesia cart he had dragged behind him into the room. "What can I do?"

Calvin answered while shucking off his bloody Patagonia vest and donning a sterile gown and gloves. "Twenty-eight-year-old, no known medical conditions or allergies, traumatic puncture to the femoral artery. Passed out from large volume blood loss. I'm about to do a vascular repair. Can you get him anesthetized so that he doesn't wake up mid-procedure?"

If they couldn't fix the leg, Yukon Valley did not have enough blood for the massive transfusion protocol. If this procedure didn't work… damn it. Deirdre clenched her hands together, hoping that anyone watching would think she was simply keeping her gloves sterile.

Tom quickly pulled medicine into syringes, labeling each one and laying them in a neat row on top of his cart. He got to work pushing meds, intubating Tuli, and hooking him up to the ER ventilator.

Dr. Yang turned to talk to someone off screen. "Yes, hold my next case. I'm going to be a while." She glanced back to the scene. "Do you have vascular clamps in that kit?"

"No, this is a laceration tray," Calvin said. "Before staff runs down to the OR, are there other surgical tools you want us to use?"

Dr. Yang nodded. "At least two small vascular clamps, a small Weitlaner retractor. Suction. For suture, use 4.0 Prolene if you have it. Give a dose of Ancef because—"

"Surgeons love Ancef?" Calvin interrupted.

"You're not wrong." Dr. Yang gave a dry chuckle.

"I'll be back in a sec." Amberlyn dashed out the door, past Mav and Louise who still hovered nearby with twin worried expressions.

Clyde said, "How much Ancef do you want?"

"Two grams," Calvin and Dr. Yang said at the same time.

In spite of her fear, Deirdre broke the tension. "Look at

you, Calvin Garrett, junior surgeon. Pretty soon that will be the only antibiotic you'll use."

Calvin rifled through the laceration tray and ripped open the chlorhexidine swab packets. He called over his shoulder, "Any issue with me scrubbing the hell out of this area?"

Dr. Yang nodded. "Scrub away. You've got plenty of time. Besides, the IV antibiotics will take care of any remaining bacteria before this patient reaches Fairbanks."

"I don't feel like I have time, Doc."

"You could keep that tourniquet on for hours or more, if you had to. There's some collateral blood flow to the leg from the profunda femoral artery, which doesn't look like it was torn."

Calvin grunted agreement. "Do we have an updated set of vitals?" He cleaned the surgical site and the surrounding area, smearing blood and cleaning solution with the sponge on an applicator stick.

Tom hit some buttons on the monitor. "Pressure ninety over fifty. Pulse one twenty. O2 sat ninety-four percent."

"ETA on blood products," Calvin asked.

The unit coordinator murmured into the phone, "Five more minutes for two crossmatched units."

Clyde held up two bags. "Or you can use these O negatives right now."

"Dr. Yang?" Calvin glanced up at the camera.

"I think we're okay to wait for typed blood. Believe it or not, you really do have some time to work with."

Clyde called out, "I'll hang the crossmatched blood when it gets here."

Calvin looked at Deirdre. "Are you ready?"

Her hands shook. Her heart drummed in her chest. But by God, if Calvin needed her help, she was going to do whatever it took to help him save Tuli's life. "Yes." She draped the field with sterile towels Clyde partially unwrapped for her to pluck from the packaging.

Amberlyn returned another few minutes later with more materials. "Got the extra equipment." With loud crackles of sterile wrapping, she opened the packs and dropped the metal devices onto the tray.

Dr. Yang peered at the screen. "Cal, go ahead and start like you would for a vascular cut-down procedure. Make it a generous incision. Give yourself some extra room to operate."

"Thanks." Calvin's neck muscles flexed as he worked. His lower face was covered by the mask. "Then use the Weitlaner to visualize the vessel for clamping?"

"Yes, basically. Your first job is to get as much exposure as possible. Don't be shy about extending farther than you think you need to go. You need to see both ends of that cut artery."

Deirdre gulped in the now-silent room as Calvin tried to place the retractor into the small puncture opening. It didn't fit. He shook his head, then took the number ten blade and extended the area several more centimeters down and up from the injury. The extra space allowed him to insert the self-retaining retractor.

Despite the tourniquet, fresh blood oozed, and Deirdre dabbed with gauze. Her back-aching position leaning over the bed was OSHA nonstandard for workplace ergonomics. No way would she complain, given the situation.

Clyde adjusted the overhead light then stepped back.

The only sound was that of the ventilator's regular whoosh and click.

Deirdre glimpsed the damaged femoral artery as she swiped away more blood. It was a thick-walled vessel with ragged edges torn completely apart and leaking blood. "I see it!"

"Good job," Calvin murmured, his praise creating a different warmth in her chest.

Dr. Yang said, "Try to get that proximal femoral artery with a vascular clamp."

Calvin tried, but he had an awkward angle. "Deirdre, can you get it from your side?"

"Yes, I think. I can. Hold on a moment…" A dull metal click sounded as she carefully locked the clamp around the artery. "There. How's that look?"

Calvin flashed a smile at her. "You're hired. Let's do the same with the distal artery." He locked the ratchets of the second vascular clamp with a metal clink. "Both are in place."

Deirdre paused. What if they fixed the damaged vessel but Tuli lost function of his leg? Or got an infection? Or required amputation? A wave of panic rushed up from the depths of her belly.

No, Deirdre wouldn't think beyond fixing the present injury.

Dr. Yang said, "Describe to me what you see in terms of

the vasculature between those two clamps."

Deirdre dabbed with a sterile swab while Calvin examined the blood vessel.

"Femoral artery is in two pieces." He pulled gently on the damaged vessel edges with forceps. "There's some play in the vessel."

"We can work with that." Dr. Yang's words seemed to infuse hope in the situation. "What you'll want to do is place interrupted sutures to reapproximate the ends of the vessel. It's either that or a graft, which I don't recommend attempting out there. Can you do the primary repair?"

Calvin tugged the vessel edges, and they met in the middle. "Yes, I think I can do it."

"First, release the lower clamp and shoot some heparinized saline down the distal vessel to keep it open and reduce clots," Dr. Yang said.

A few moves later and Calvin looked up. "Done and reclamped."

"Blood's here, Doc," Clyde said. "I'm running the first unit wide open and the second over an hour if that sounds okay."

"Yes, great idea." He continued to examine the damaged artery.

Deirdre tried to anticipate his movements with retractors and gauze. "How else can I help you?" she murmured.

"You're doing so well." Lines crinkled at the edges of his gray eyes as he glanced at her. "Does this count as our first date?" He pitched his voice low.

A brief wave of warmth flowed from her toes to her head

as she resisted checking to see if anyone noticed. "Ha. Hope not."

Turning back to the tray, he selected a suture, loaded the needle on the driver, and placed the first stitch. Sweat glistened on his forehead. With a few flicks of the instruments, he tied a knot and gingerly tugged on it.

The suture held.

Deirdre threw up a thanks to the heavens and snipped the suture.

For the next fifteen minutes, Calvin painstakingly placed fine, closely spaced sutures, tying each one individually.

Once he was done, he said, "I think we're good. Do I need additional stitches for reinforcement?"

Dr. Yang shook her head. "If you feel like you have a solid line of suture, then release the distal clamp slightly and see if the repair holds under a small amount of backflow."

The room was dead silent except for the beeps of the monitor and the sounds of the ventilator keeping Tuli alive while Calvin worked. He carefully opened the clamp, and the vessel slowly expanded. No oozing around the suture site. No pooling in the surgical field.

Had this amazing physician actually repaired a femoral artery at the bedside?

Deirdre stared at the vessel as if she could hold it together by sheer force of will.

"Now for the moment of truth," Dr. Yang said. "Release the proximal vascular clamp."

"I really don't want to do that," Calvin said in a droll tone.

Deirdre snorted but gently rested her gloved hand on his. "You've got this."

Calvin took a deep breath. "Here goes nothing."

Chapter Eight

C AL SLIPPED TWO uncharacteristically shaking fingers in
the rings of the clamp on the femoral artery above his
repair and slowly released pressure. *Please work*, he prayed.
Worst came to worst, he could re-clamp everything and
hope they could get Tuli to Fairbanks in under twenty-four
hours. They'd be racing the clock against permanent tissue
damage and an entire blizzard, but at least he had a plan B,
even if it semi-sucked.

The artery below the clamp filled with blood, even with
the tourniquet still applied on Tuli's upper thigh.

Then a pulse became visible. Each jump of the vessel sent
a jolt of adrenaline through his own circulation.

Hold. Hold.

Three more pulsations. He expected to see blood squirt-
ing from between the sutures.

He gritted his teeth. *Hold, goddammit.*

"Can you dab that area, please?" His voice came out
shaky. Hopefully no one noticed or thought poorly of him
for it.

"To be honest, I don't want to touch it," Deirdre said.

Despite the situation, he chuckled. She didn't realize
how much her quiet confidence grounded him in this

situation.

"Hey, I don't blame you one bit." He met her bright blue stare, and the tension between his shoulder blades eased. "But we have to."

She dabbed the suture line and surrounding tissue. No bleeding from the vessel. Only a small amount of oozing came from damaged but now re-perfused muscle. His heart lodged in his throat. Had they really done it? "I think it's good."

"Way to go. You might make a solid surgery intern before you're all done." Dr. Yang laughed. As everyone in the room took a deep breath, Dr. Yang intoned, "You're not quite done. The location of injury has a high risk of tearing the nearby femoral vein and femoral nerve. See if you can isolate and check those structures."

He and Deirdre both sucked in twin deep breaths and bent their heads in unison, studying the exposed tissue. The vein was lateral to the artery and—he carefully dissected around it enough to visualize it and gingerly move it with vascular forceps—patent. The nerve? He found a remnant of the off-white millimeter thick nerve below the injury site. Torn.

"Where's the other part?" he muttered.

Deirdre dabbed and gently pushed tissue back. "Is that it?"

He blinked, willing himself not to anchor his conclusion in the first structure he saw that looked like a nerve. He forced himself to go through the process of looking around and considering what else this could represent. It did look like a nerve. Tracing it proximally a few centimeters, he identified the muscular branches of the nerve. Likely above that, it would come together into the thick main femoral nerve.

Okay. He had both ends of the severed nerve. "Found it, Dr. Yang."

"If you can reapproximate the endings of that nerve with a stitch, that will reduce the chance of long-term neurological damage to the limb."

He lifted his hand, wanting to brush sweat from his forehead, but caught himself. There really should be a surgeon here in Yukon Valley twenty-four seven for times like this.

Bending to the task, he placed two sutures into the ends of the severed nerve and snugged them together. "Done."

"Give the area some good irrigation to make sure you remove any foreign material."

Deirdre dabbed as he drew up sterile saline in a large syringe and flushed the area several times. The fluid soaked the sterile towels and the bed. A mixture of blood and saline dripped off the vinyl mattress and onto the floor.

"This room looks like a disaster, but the wound, I think, is cleaned out," he said.

Deirdre's eyes lit up. "I'll run interference for complaints from environmental services staff when they try to clean this mess."

Everyone chuckled. The air in the room seemed less heavy.

Dr. Yang said, "Only thing left to do is release the tourniquet."

Cal locked onto Deirdre's wide-eyed stare. "I am one hundred percent certain none of us want to do that, Dr. Yang."

"I know. But do it."

"All right. Moment of truth. Clyde, can you reach under the sterile towel and loosen the tourniquet?"

Clyde slowly released the pressure. As blood flowed, completely unimpeded, through the leg, the femoral pulse bounded more vigorously, and the surrounding tissue and distal limb went from pallor to pink in a matter of a few minutes.

"I'll be darned." Cal said, then caught himself. "Um, not that I had any doubt whatsoever this would totally work." He whipped his head around to shoot daggers at the snickering staff.

Deirdre said, "You did it!" Her smile was hidden by the mask, but he could see the happy crinkles next to her eyes.

Dr. Yang interrupted the celebrations. "Great job and all that jazz. All right, friends. Some of us have work to do," she said dryly. "Irrigate a few more times, then close the defect. Don't worry about layered closure. Place a pressure dressing over the site. Ship him as soon as you are able, and we'll be ready for him whenever he arrives. We'll do follow-up management up here."

"Dr. Yang. Fantastic assist from hundreds of miles away. We can't thank you enough." Cal blew out a huge breath. "Now I know why I'm getting gray hair."

"You earned every strand." Deirdre's confident tone of

voice warmed him.

The staff disconnected the telehealth unit and rolled it out of the room. Tuli's vitals were stable. The second unit of blood dripped through the IV.

After another ten minutes of irrigation and additional repair, Calvin stood up straight, every muscle and joint protesting the upright position.

Sure, he managed plenty of life-threatening situations on a regular basis at Harborview.

Never without a safety net.

Yukon Valley Hospital might be small, but the staff and their ability to improvise was next level.

After taking off his gown, gloves, eye shields, and mask, he said, "Everyone did an impressive job saving Tuli's life. Way to go. Let's do a team debrief before shift change." He took a moment to meet everyone's eyes. "But bottom line for me is that I couldn't have done this without every one of you here today." He stopped rotating when he got to Deirdre. Her steady encouragement made him feel like he could save any patient, regardless of how few resources were available.

He could get used to unwavering support like that. A dangerous thought.

Deirdre smiled at Cal and the team, faint red lines marking her cheeks and the bridge of her nose where the mask had rested. "I'd give everyone a hug, but I'm a total disaster." She paused, her gaze raking over him. "And Dr. Garrett looks like he committed a crime!"

"My only crime is doing surgery without an actual license." The laugh that came up from the depths of his belly released the past hour of tension like a popped balloon. "I'm counting on the fact that no one is going to report me to the state medical board." Of course, he was covered by the fact that he was working within his scope as an ED physician, but everyone seemed to appreciate the levity of the moment.

Ducking out to the call room, he quickly rinsed off in the shower, grabbed a fresh pair of underwear and socks and a T-shirt, and threw on clean scrubs. In a matter of minutes, he had holding orders placed and a plan for transfer to Fairbanks as soon as the weather would allow.

Staff cleaned up the mess in the room and began restocking supplies, their companionable murmurs wrapping around him. Deirdre had stuck around to help Amberlyn and Clyde.

Deirdre was something else. Cool under pressure. Confident. A perfect partner.

For someone else. He scrubbed his eyelids, as if that would get the image of her wide blue eyes out of his memory.

Fifteen minutes later, Tom stuck his head out of the trauma bay. "Tuli's awake now, Doc."

As Cal stepped into the room, Tuli gave a groggy smile. "Hey, Doc. I made it. Either that or heaven is not as advertised." He glanced toward the door, then down at his bloody bed linens and clothes. "Hi, Lou. Sorry my artery attacked you and made the inside of the ambulance look like an exorcism occurred. Any chance I can get cleaned up?"

Mav snorted as he rolled the gurney away toward the ambulance bay.

Louise smiled, brows furrowed. "We'll be cleaning the rig for a week. You, too, from the looks of it. Ah, Clyde's got you a fresh gown and sheets." With another long look, she pushed off the open sliding doorway and followed Maverick out.

"Hey, someone give me my phone. I'm going live before I put that pastel blue gown on." Tuli snorted. "Bet this story will go viral."

Everyone in the room eye-rolled or groaned. No one handed him his phone.

Cal squeezed Tuli's upper arm, turned around, and spied Deirdre gingerly picking up her clean blazer from the countertop. The front of her blouse had a dark stain on it from Tuli's blood. Tendrils of sweaty hair had matted on her neck and cheeks. Her face was still flushed, probably from the heat of wearing the impermeable gown while working under the bright exam light.

Hardworking. Determined. Endearing.

Beautiful.

"I'm heading out, unless anybody needs anything else." Deirdre shoved hair behind an ear.

When she paused a few feet from Cal, everything else in the room faded away. Dimly, he noted that the staff had made themselves very busy or very scarce.

"Thanks again, Deirdre."

"I'd say *anytime*, but no offense—I'm calling it a day and hoping no one needs me for the next twelve hours." She wrinkled her nose, smiled at everyone, then turned on her heel and exited.

For an extra few seconds, Cal stared at the sliding glass door.

"There's a problem, Doc," Tuli said.

He immediately leaned over him, lifting the fresh gown to check the dry dressing on his leg. "What? Are you in pain? Any breathing issues?"

"No. You have it bad." Maybe the blood loss caused confusion.

"What?"

"Look, I might have been under anesthesia, but I have enough brain cells left to tell me what saw." He pursed his lips. "You in denial about Deirdre Steen?"

His neck prickled as his stomach took a dive. "First of all, there's nothing going on. Second of all"—he glanced toward the door where Louise hovered, ostensibly finishing up paperwork—"you have zero room to talk. Do you want me to go into detail with my *lucid* observations about you making eyes at a certain EMT?"

Tuli started to cross his arms but winced at the IVs and straightened his limbs out again. His eyes went wide, then shuttered. "Yep, must be the drugs making me see and say silly things. Forget I said anything. Never mind."

Two could play this game. "That's what I thought."

Exiting the trauma bay, Cal settled in front of a computer in the work area to finish his documentation and add any other orders. On his phone resting next to the monitor, he glanced at a red notification. His shoulders tightened. He had been expecting an email that could disrupt everything, whether he wanted it to or not.

As the message popped up, he blew out a breath and sank down in the seat. It was from his department chair at Harborview, checking in on his timeline for returning. Of course they needed him there, covering shifts. He knew his absence had created a hardship for the team.

What of his absence from the team here?

What about his absence from the person who made the best team with Cal? Who always had.

Scrubbing his hands over his face for what had to be the thousandth time today, Cal turned the phone facedown. He had an entire career waiting for him back in Seattle.

He had … appearances to maintain in Yukon Valley.

This work, these friends, playing pretend with Deirdre— all of it was temporary. A foundation built on melting ice.

For some reason, Calvin wasn't prepared to sink or drown.

Chapter Nine

A DAY LATER, on Tuesday evening and the first day of April, Deirdre took a shaky breath as Calvin pulled up in his gray mud-and-slush spattered rental sedan in front of her home. Showtime.

Tuli had been transferred to Fairbanks late this morning when the weather finally broke. He was reportedly stable and undergoing additional surgery and testing.

Before he left, Tuli apparently had recovered enough blood volume to power both brain and mouth if his social media posts were any indication. He rode a wave of renewed energy, even convening an ad hoc Breakup Festival's hospice booth subcommittee in his ED room at morning shift change.

He and the committee members assigned jobs for the hospital leaders at the Breakup Festival. She'd known because she had attended the meeting.

When he'd dangled the possibility of Deirdre staffing a kissing booth, he and the bedside nurse had laughed a bit too long. Deirdre needed to pretend, but hello? How about some boundaries from her coworkers.

Boundaries? No.

Relentless pressure? Yes.

So, Deirdre had volunteered for the snow-pie-in-the-face booth instead.

At least she hadn't been assigned to the ice water dunk for hospice like Calvin.

She shuddered as she gripped the back of her couch. Nothing could compel her to go into a tank of ice water. Not for a good cause. Not even in a safe, controlled environment.

A wave of air-stealing grief from her parents' watery death hit her out of the blue.

She couldn't breathe.

Their crashed plane through the ice. Frigid water, suffocating them.

Every part of her body dropped ten degrees.

The doorbell rang, jolting her back to reality. She rubbed her cold arms through the light pink sweater. Deirdre had barely made it home from a long day at work in time to change for tonight's *date*.

Finally. A public, fake date so they could both appease the relentlessly helpful family and friends.

She glanced over at patterned couch in her living room. The room was too large for one person. The furniture was too much for one person. A framed picture caught her eye, and she swallowed a lump in her throat as she tossed up a silent apology to Elijah as she gently tucked the picture in her top desk drawer.

Crossing back across the living room was a long-distance journey filled with unknown dangers and an uncertain destination. Her well-ordered and insulated world shifted, and she scuffed a foot on the carpet, trying to regain her balance.

Reaching for the doorknob felt like a huge step. A turning point. A deliberate decision.

No. She shook her head. This was just dinner with a friend she was pretending to date. A mutually beneficial and pleasant smokescreen.

She swung the door open, and Deirdre's mouth dropped. True to weather changes in spring, last night's blizzard had given way to an afternoon of temperatures in the forties and melting snow. As such, Calvin didn't have on a coat. He wore a plaid green button-down with the top button open enough to show a small dusting of dark hair. Over the shirt was a black Patagonia vest. His shoulders filled out the garments well.

Deirdre rolled her hands into loose fists, resisting the urge to pat his chest and discover how he felt under those clothes. She knew she'd find his warm, lean, solid frame beneath her fingertips. She swallowed.

Every hair on his head was in place. He wore black hiking pants, the trim waistband hinted at what lay beneath the hem of the vest.

She inhaled, catching a scent of soap and spicy aftershave, which led her to examine his smooth jaw. Unconsciously, she leaned toward him, then caught herself with a startle.

"Hello," she managed to stammer.

"You look great, Deirdre." His voice rumbled through her, sending a tingle down her legs. "I mean, you always look great. But you look casually great today." He frowned. "But not too casual. Socially appropriate. Unlike work attire. Which is also socially appropriate. Uh."

In spite of herself, she laughed, a broad, loud sound that came up from a source of pure joy. She hadn't done that in such a long time. "You look nice, too." In those hiking pants and flannel shirt and vest, he looked good enough to snuggle into. "Glad I'm not the only awkward one here."

"Oh, that smooth bit?" He shrugged. "I was just breaking the ice."

"As one does in Yukon Valley."

His wide grin set her back on her heels. "Touché." Leaning against the doorframe, he said, "Ready to make us Yukon Valley official?"

"Let's walk the plank."

"We'll walk it together." He pretended to tug at his collar, took her hand.

Peering up at him, she asked, "Bruce and Aggie nagging at you?"

"You have no idea. They're in cahoots with the hospital staff's matchmakers."

"The staff is relentless. I got all kinds of hints about how well we worked together yesterday."

"We did. Professionally speaking."

"Exactly." Somehow her agreement felt a half degree off plumb. "When I tried to refocus their attention elsewhere, they keep circling back. They're like lynxes, able to stalk a topic for hours at a time."

"They work fast to set people up."

"I wish they'd do their quarterly training modules as quickly."

The low bark of his laugh caught her off guard, but she chuckled along with him.

"Always the administrator," he said.

She shot him a grin as he helped her shrug into her light coat. "Sure." Stopping, she asked, "Hey, any recent updates on Tuli?"

His warm smile melted her insides. "I spoke with Dr. Yang right before I got here. They had brought him back from the OR where they had performed a second cleanout of the wound. She said our repair was solid."

"*Your* repair. I only dabbed and cut suture."

"Oh no, that was a full-contact team sport yesterday in the ER." He waited while she locked the door. Unnecessary in this tight-knit community but a good habit for safety. "They cauterized small arteriolar bleeds in the area and did extra microsurgical work on the femoral nerve that had been severed."

"Will he have a limp or sensation issues?"

"Initially, probably. But physical therapy should help him recover. How much, we don't know. It'll take time to see how he does."

"Well, at least he's in good hands for the best chance of recovery." Pocketing the keys, she turned to him. "Um. So."

He tugged her away from the entrance and waved at no less than three neighbors peeking out their windows or front doors. In the twilight, silhouettes were clear with lamplight behind them. "Let's do this right." He drew her hand up to his mouth and pressed a kiss over her knuckles.

Deirdre giggled.

What the heck? Giggled? She hadn't giggled since …

A prick of pain to her chest came and went.

Far too long.

It was long past time for more giggling.

He held out his arm, and Deirdre looped her hand in the crook of his elbow. Such a simple act, but it came with a flood of emotions that she was not prepared to explore.

Dinner with a friend.

A little show for folks in town so they'd let up on the matchmaking efforts.

Curiosity appeased. Gossip fodder controlled and directed. Social pressure removed.

Everyone would win.

He handed her into the car, and they drove three minutes to the local diner, eventually sitting at a table by the window. Not Deirdre's choice of location.

"Maximum exposure," Calvin explained.

"Because everyone craning their necks in here won't give us exposure enough?"

Deirdre waved at Gordy Wright, who was having dinner with his parents. His big lopsided grin and jerky wave spoke to the developmental delays and physical challenges he'd had growing up. The whole town knew and loved Gordy. His younger sister, Louise, one of the town's EMT's, wasn't with the family this evening.

"Hey, Gordy," Calvin called out, and the young man gave a yelping laugh, extra loud in the diner. No one seemed to be bothered. "You staying out of trouble?"

Gordy shook his head and made a choppy *no way* sign. With smiles and murmurs, his parents drew him back to his dinner.

Calvin turned to Deirdre. "Good to know some things haven't changed even after all these years." He lowered his voice and leaned forward. "Although Mom was saying that he's slowed down a bit."

Deirdre nodded. "Still going like the Energizer bunny. Gordy's an institution. Always has been. As soon as the weather gets better, he'll have his safety jacket for his daily rounds walking around town, checking in at every store and stopping by the hospital for a lap or two inside. Seems like he conveniently ends up at the hospital right at lunch time. And just as conveniently, Chef Luka has a sandwich cut up into small pieces, ready to go."

Calvin chuckled until the waitress arrived to take their orders. Leaning back in the seat, he crossed his arms and exhaled. "Mom's cooking is great, and my frozen meals in the hospital's rental are fine, but a meal out at the Yukon Diner is a treat."

"I'll say."

"Do you get out much?"

Her face warmed. "Too busy with the hospital and the lodge. There's always something going on, it seems."

"You haven't had another reason to go out for a nice meal?"

"Are you prying?"

"I mean, we *are* fake-dating. We should get to know each

other better."

"Seriously. We know each other too well." Which might be the problem. Deirdre toyed with her water, her thumb encouraging a drop of water to slide down the side of the glass. "Things have been different since ... Elijah passed away. You know?"

"I can imagine."

A bitter taste coated her tongue. Calvin hadn't been around from the time he left for college until now. Except for a few quick visits with his parents and the time when he visited Elijah in hospice, which she figured had been an obligation. He certainly hadn't reached out to her over the years. But she wouldn't judge. People had their own lives and their own way of dealing with grief.

"He was a great guy." Calvin's gaze slid off toward the window. "You two were the perfect couple."

An invisible knife twisted in her chest. "The three of us were such good friends, back in the day."

"I miss those times."

"Me too."

She swallowed a hard lump, needing to redirect the conversation before a wave of grief embarrassed her. "Hey, my brother might be a stinker at times, but Mav's been helpful over the years."

A gentle smile crinkled lines around his thoughtful gray eyes. "Maverick's good people. Most folks around here are." His gaze turned serious as he leaned forward, elbows on the table. "Listen, I wanted to let you know that I'm sorry. I should have been here more. During Elijah's illness and afterward. It was … time and work and all."

"You don't have to explain your obligations to me, Calvin."

"I don't have to explain avoidance to you, either."

"Ouch."

A wry twist lifted one side of his mouth. "Hey, I was talking about me." He spread his hands and arms wide. "Exhibit A. This dinner. A monument to Avoidance 101. Hey, cheers to our teamwork." He lifted the amber beer, and she clinked her water glass against his.

"That's funny." She took a sip. It would have been wonderful to have an IPA, but she wanted to be totally clearheaded this evening. "Have you thought about for-real seeing anyone?" She paused. "Oh, that's presumptuous of me. You might already be doing that in Seattle."

"First of all, I wouldn't have agreed to our deal if I was in a current relationship." He lifted one finger then two. "Second of all, I could ask you the same question. Why aren't you dating? It's been five years since Elijah passed."

Her tongue stuck to the roof of her mouth. "It's a small town. Work and the lodge keep me busy."

"That's not an answer." He rested his fingertips on the back of her hand.

The truth was too close to speak the words. "It's the answer I am able to give." She rotated her hand, so his fingers nestled in her palm. Tingles coursed up her arm. She swallowed and slid her hand away and into her lap.

He studied her for several long seconds—enough to make her heart flop beneath her ribs. "I noticed you changed your last name back."

A nod. "Last year. Finally. Felt like I was ready for that step."

"Good for you."

Time to bail out of this topic and fast. She dropped her voice, ensuring no one could overhear. "Hey, great job with Tuli yesterday. That was some neat work you did."

He paused. "*Hmmph.* Good conversation dodge. Fine, I'll play along." Drawing a hand over his face, he shook his head. "That was hairier than I had wanted to manage. Glad he's doing better today. I don't think I mentioned it, but Fairbanks was running a CT angiogram as well this evening."

"At least they know what to watch for and can fix any issues right away."

He nodded. "The part Tuli won't like will be the light duty for at least eight weeks. No lifting or exertion." He paused, brows drawn together. "If he has lingering issues related to the femoral nerve damage as well? His job may need to change."

"That's going to be a tough road, what with his work as a firefighter."

"Knowing Tuli, he's the Fire Chief. He can easily shift into a fully admin role where he gets to show up and direct everyone around him."

Deirdre laughed. "Organizing and assigning tasks? That's on brand."

"He's still making eyes at Louise?"

"See, now there's a worthy matchmaking project the town and the hospital staff should get behind."

JILLIAN DAVID

"It's an obvious pair. Not sure why they haven't gotten together yet." He shrugged. "At the end of the day, it's not my business. I know what it's like to be under the social microscope. Those two have to figure things out for themselves." He glanced up as an older couple got up to leave, and he nodded at them. "I do vaguely remember Tuli and Louise being friends in school. He always looked out for her."

"They were in sixth grade when you were a senior in high school. How did you know?"

"I know all about childhood sw—" He cleared his throat. "You realize that this is a ridiculously small town, right? My parents keep me updated on their observations and every last bit of the gossip."

Deirdre turned her head as someone coughed at one of the tables, then focused on Calvin. "In general, everyone knows way too much about everyone. Getting into people's business is like the town hobby." She sighed. "In good news, we do have some influx of non-Yukon Valley born population from time to time, what with the Alaska Fish and Game office in town. Folks in town are developing tourism offerings, like we are with our lodge. The Yukon River recreation activities and the corporation's new Koyukon Athabascan cultural center also bring tourists to the area."

"Not to mention dogsledding, right?"

"Hopefully, we can increase the interest in recreational dogsledding, yes. Take advantage of the Iditarod publicity each winter."

Food came, and they tucked into a few bites of meatloaf

for Calvin and battered halibut for Deirdre. When had she last had a nice meal out like this? Far too long.

He swallowed his bite and took a sip of his beer. "I'm glad your lodge business is coming along. I heard about the stupidity Maverick and Lee—and you—had to deal with."

"Those investors were real snakes," she hissed.

His flinch surprised her, but he recovered. "Glad they're gone."

That was a bland answer, but she nodded. "You don't see Mav mad much. He made an exception for those jerks when they tried to push us into foreclosure."

"That's wild."

"I'll say." She set down her fork. "Mom and Dad never let on that the property had any value beyond the acreage and the lodge. I don't think they knew. Mav and I certainly had no idea about the ores and rare earth minerals on our land."

"What are you going to do with that information?"

"Why? You looking to invest?"

He pulled his head back and lifted a hand and a fork. "No, but I'm wondering about my parents. Mom and Pop's property lies on the Ray Mountain range as does the Koyukon village land. The question is, how can we keep those outsiders from being a nuisance? If they're determined, then they will find a way to gain access."

"Mav and your dad were talking strategy the other day. The Alaska Department of Natural Resources and the Bureau of Land Management could issue a mining permit for a prospector to access BLM-managed land. The entire

Ray Mountain range is managed by BLM. But Yukon Valley's citizens own all of the access to the mountains. It's prohibitive for someone to go around our collective property to reach the ore. For example, if Randy Nelson picked up our land, he'd have an easy straight shot across the meadow to the base of the range. Right now, he would have to go over and around the Yukon River, and that's a massive and expensive engineering feat."

Calvin nodded. "If there's going to be any extraction, it should be the way folks here feel is best. Ensure that it's done right. Pay a reasonable price for the access."

"Where did that come from? All of a sudden you sound like an old timer here!"

"Probably have some of Pop rubbing off on me."

She laughed. "Ol' Bruce is so stubborn, he won't sell."

"Funny, but I'm trying to get him to do exactly that. For his health. Get him to move somewhere better suited."

A twinge hit her, unrelated to the unscrupulous investors. "Your dad won't leave."

"Despite my best efforts."

Another barking sound came from a few tables over. "Well, I—"

"Gordy?" his mother's voice rose. "Gordy, are you okay? Steve, lay him on the floor so he doesn't get injured."

Deirdre pushed her plate forward and stood up. "Melinda, you need help?"

"No, we're fine—" She and her husband struggled to carefully ease Gordy to the floor. Jerking movements and a twisting flexion of his hands, arms, and wrists told the tale of his seizure.

Deirdre strode over. "Let me help." She tugged on Gordy's thin shoulders and eased him to his side in a recovery position. "I don't remember if this is his usual routine."

Calvin knelt and checked Gordy's pulse, scanning the young man's shaking frame.

Sitting next to his son, Steve glanced at his wife and then to Deirdre. "He generally has a light seizure then comes right out of it."

Melinda added, "The pattern has been changing lately. More frequent and severe seizures. Dr. Burmeister and the tele-neurologist were adjusting his medications over the last few weeks."

Gordy continued the tonic-clonic seizure for another twenty seconds, without abating.

Deirdre called to the waitress from where she knelt on the floor. "Could you get EMS here, please? He may need to go to the ED." The bluish tinge to his lips worried her. Transient drops in oxygen were normal in seizures but could become dangerous if the seizure didn't stop.

Calvin swiped some napkins from an empty table and gently wiped saliva and food from Gordy's mouth. The diner owner rushed out with clean towels to use. Calvin kept a loose, protective hand beneath Gordy's head so he wouldn't hurt himself. Fishing out his phone from his pants pocket, he hit a number. "Hi, Lee, it's Cal. Gordy Wright is headed your way with what looks like a grand mal seizure. Intractable. No vitals at this time. I'll direct EMS to give some lorazepam when they get here. Yeah. Okay, we'll see you in a bit."

Deirdre tried to reassure Steve and Melinda while keeping Gordy on his side. There was Calvin, calling in report to the on-call doc, making sure the ED was prepared for the patient.

The front door clanked and EMTs Hilda and Moose rolled in, quickly applied oxygen and EKG leads while Deirdre placed an IV. Hilda then gave a dose of lorazepam at Calvin's direction. Once the seizure subsided, they carefully transferred Gordy onto the lowered gurney. His respirations had a gurgling quality to them, alarming to hear but typical in a post-seizure state.

Melinda and Steve collected their coats and followed the gurney to the front door.

"Hey, Melinda," Deirdre called out. "Leave me your keys. You two go with him. I'll drop your car off at the hospital in a little bit."

Chapter Ten

CAL HELPED DEIRDRE and the waitress clean the floor, then he washed up in the restroom and met her back at the table. Her steady, blue gaze connected with him, and she gave a brief smile that triggered a warm thump in his chest.

Deirdre had jumped in without hesitation to help Gordy.

Any healthcare worker, Cal included, would do the same in a similar situation. But the way she soothed an unconscious, seizing Gordy while comforting the parents, triggered a memory of Deirdre, with a gentle and tired smile, taking steady care of Elijah while he was in hospice. More memories surfaced of Deirdre patching up Cal or Elijah when they screwed up on any number of youthful dares so many years ago.

The constant was Deirdre. She was always there.

At her heart she was a caregiver, ready to help. Never not on duty. Kindhearted, practical, and emotionally sturdy. Cal had never given it much thought. Her care was a given. She'd always been that way.

The reality hit harder now. He knew the nuts and bolts of the caregiver role from his medical experience. However, he had a much better idea of what it took to be a caregiver, since he was dipping toe into that job with his parents. Still, what he dealt with was nothing compared with what Deirdre had done on a daily basis.

What she continued to do on a daily basis.

His gut tightened as he studied her profile as she looked out of the diner window, one hand pressed to the tabletop. A line formed between her brows. He wanted to smooth it away with his finger. Share some of her burdens. Take them off her shoulders, at least for a time. He rocked back on his heels.

No way would he explore this new feeling, because that meant he would have to expose something new and uncomfortable about himself.

"Want a to-go box?" he said, voice coming out hoarse.

Brown eyebrows rose briefly, and she pulled her head back. "Oh. Yes, that's probably the right thing to do." She sighed.

"Sorry that dinner was interrupted."

"Not your fault. I'm glad we were here to help."

"Very true," he mumbled. He held her coat as she slid her arms in, then went to the register.

"No charge for you two." The waitress crossed her arms.

"We can pay for our dinner," he insisted.

The waitress lifted her chin to the owner, who had been helping with other customers while EMS had attended to Gordy.

"Sorry, folks," the owner said with a wide smile. "Your money's no good here this evening."

"Again, not necessary." He glanced at the lifting corners

of Deirdre's mouth. "But thank you."

Deirdre echoed her thanks as they exited.

They crunched in slushy snow to Melinda's car, and he held the door open. "I'll follow you to the hospital."

"So much for a first date." She stood on the other side of the door, shoulders sagged. Always on duty.

He gripped the bags of food he held, the movement preventing him from wrapping his arms around her. "At least we got our public appearance taken care of."

"Appearance. That's right." Her gaze slid off of him and away. "Finally."

After they parked both his vehicle and Melinda's in front of the hospital, he and Deirdre badged through the emergency department entrance and stepped into the ED room the unit coordinator at the work area desk indicated.

"Melinda?" Deirdre said softly.

Gordy's parents looked up from their seats at his bedside. He slept soundly, his normally tight limbs limp, a light gurgling snore coming with each breath. Cal couldn't resist checking the vitals on the monitor. Sats were ninety-five percent on oxymask, pulse regular, blood pressure soft but probably okay given Gordy's age around thirty and condition.

With a quick hug around the neck to both of them, Deirdre handed over the keys. "He's sleeping hard, huh?"

Melinda nodded, lines of fatigue and age etching her kind face. "With the combination of a post-seizure state and the lorazepam, he'll be out cold for many hours."

"Anything I can do?"

Deirdre rested a hand on the woman's shoulder. Suddenly, Cal felt like a real outsider. Like he needed to slip out of the room. He edged toward the door.

"Thank you, but we're good. This is par for the course with our Gordy. Dr. Tipton said he should stay for observation. She wants to watch for more seizures in case this is a cluster. He also needs treatment with antibiotics for aspiration."

"Yes, that was a long seizure," Deirdre said in a soft voice, like she wanted to agree but didn't want to say too much.

Steve and Melinda locked eyes. "Sure was," he said with a grimace. "But Gordy keeps trucking along, right, hon?"

"What other option is there?" Melinda's smile was sad. "Besides, we were due for another family health issue."

Another issue? Cal racked his brain. He didn't know Melinda and Steve well, as they were about thirteen years older than him. He hadn't heard that they were ill. Their daughter Louise? She seemed healthy.

What did he know? No surprise there were things going on in town that he hadn't been aware of. Why that bothered him, he couldn't say.

Deirdre gave one more pat on the shoulder and stepped back. "Well, let me know what I can do to help."

"You're in great hands tonight," Cal added. "Dr. Tipton is an excellent physician. And it looks like Gordy's stabilized."

"Of course," Melinda said. "The joke in our family is that with all the health issues his entire life, Gordy must have nine lives."

Steve snorted. "He might have nine lives, but I'm personally down to seven after tonight's seizure."

They all laughed softly. Cal and Deirdre exited the room.

Cal stopped at the work area next to Lee Tipton, family physician and newcomer to Yukon Valley. "Feeling good about Gordy?" he asked.

Dr. Tipton was an excellent physician, but she fully acknowledged that she hadn't done inpatient or ED work in several years. When she asked him questions, it was obvious to Cal the exercise was for confirmation, not direction. She knew her stuff and only needed reinforcement that her decisions were sound.

"Thanks for checking. Seizure med levels are pending, and I'll adjust the dose if need be. Ativan as needed overnight. Labs and cultures cooking. The chest x-ray had some infiltrates, so I'm covering for pneumonia. Not sure if he was getting ill and that's what triggered the seizure or if he had the seizure and then aspirated."

"Chicken and the egg, huh?"

"At this point, the treatment's the same."

"True."

"Hey, you two scoot on out of here already. You're off duty." She waved. "Hi, Deirdre! It sounded like last weekend's guests were really happy."

Deirdre smiled, and it felt like sunshine indoors to Cal. "They booked another reservation to return this fall during the salmon run!"

"That's great news!"

"More work, but that's a fabulous problem to have!" Deirdre made an exhausted face complete with panting until they all chuckled.

"Better than having a problem with the land prospectors," Lee frowned. "I hate folks who lie," Lee said, her Georgia accent always surprising to hear in Alaska. "They faked an injury so that they could sue. They're lower than a snake's belly in a ditch."

Cal clenched his hand. He hated that someone had threatened to take Deirdre and Maverick's property. Hated that they posed a safety risk to people he cared about. Hated having those people anywhere near Yukon Valley. "How'd you expose them, Lee?"

Deirdre nodded. "She heard their plan while she treated the injured man in the ED."

"Because they didn't recognize me from when I helped Maverick out in the field, because la-de-da how could *I* be a doctor, right?" She batted her long lashes. "However, as the treating ED doc, it was fair game to document the pertinent history and patient statements right into the chart!" Lee laughed. "Their case hinged on medical notes. I simply made sure the notes were thorough and accurate. If not damning."

Cal whistled low. "Never heard of weaponizing the medical record. As much as I hate documentation, I'm glad for once it was used for good not evil."

"It was a real pleasure." She waggled her fingers. "Hey, seriously, you kids get on out of here and finish your date. Have a great evening."

Deirdre's cheeks flushed red. Her mouth opened, then

closed.

The nearby unit coordinator covered a snicker. There were literally no secrets in Yukon Valley.

Cal's phone buzzed, and he glanced at the text, brows shooting up. His jaw tightened. "It's Mom and Pop. Damn it, the timing is bad. This evening keeps getting better and better." He paused to read the message again. "Mind if we swing by their place?"

"Sure thing," Deirdre said.

The ER staff definitely watched them leave.

Chapter Eleven

C AL DIDN'T WANT to speed, but Mom's text rattled him. Some man had been *poking around* the homestead. His mind immediately went to the investor. This was not how things worked in Alaska, people just showing up on someone's property and asking questions like this. Damn it.

While Mom and Pop were two of the most rugged and resourceful people Cal knew, he also understood they were vulnerable. His parents were both nearing seventy, still active, but definitely lived in a more isolated setting than Cal liked, out on the homestead. At least they had satellite internet, which meant they had phone service—an improvement from even a few years ago.

But Mom's cell phone had no signal while out on the property. No towers were close enough to their location. She could only call or text over satellite internet if they were in or near the house.

Pop had the heart issue. Damn it. Many reasons why it was time for them to move to a safer environment and a larger town with services. He pressed on the accelerator, but not enough to lose control on the slushy road.

A light touch on his hand that rested on the gear shift startled him.

"You okay?" Deirdre said.

Her fingers on the back of his hand anchored him. Calmed him. Her mere presence soothed him in ways he wouldn't fully acknowledge.

The space in this car had become way too small for both of them. He needed air. Distance. A clear head to think through this situation. He gripped the wheel and inhaled her light floral and crisp linen scent. Their stupid sham had been a mistake. He flexed his wrist, enjoying how her palm remained connected to the back of his hand.

Damn it. He should give up the fake relationship.

He had no time for this kind of situation. They had too many other priorities, like dealing with threats to their families.

He squinted through the slush-spattered windshield.

Selfishly, he enjoyed spending time with Deirdre, although he appreciated that her free time was precious and rare. She didn't need to waste it on him.

For what? He swallowed a hard lump.

Protection. Sure. Their pretend dating acted as a social heat shield for both of them. Giving even a small reprieve to the stressors in Deirdre's life—that was motivation enough for Cal to continue the charade. Not that he was rationalizing.

He turned his hand halfway over and hooked his thumb over her hand, savoring the warm connection. "Not sure. Mom sounded worried."

He turned off the state highway and traveled up a long gravel road into the hills outside of town. In the early April evening, at eight thirty, the sun had set. The snowstorm from yesterday had cleared out, revealing stars from horizon to horizon, popping up as twilight faded. This time of year, months of snow melted in the daytime and refroze again every night. Wet rocks and slushy crunches rattled under the vehicle.

Pulling up to the cabin, he scanned for anything out of place.

Nothing. No other vehicles.

He tried to see his family's home like Deirdre would. The handmade two-story cabin had repairs and additions over the years, but it was a solid structure. Lights glowed from the front windows. Off to one side was another metal building that was dark—the garage-barn-shed.

He scanned the snow, gravel, and icy mud-covered parking pad, then studied the spruces protecting the north and west of the house—a necessary windbreak in this area. Opposite the windbreaks, hills covered in low pines and leafless deciduous trees rolled back down toward town and the river.

He got out and came around to Deirdre's side of car, helping her out. He winced as her booties, more fashionable than functional, squelched in the messy mixture underfoot. Keeping a hand under her arm, they walked up a few porch steps to the front door, which opened right as he lifted his hand to knock. Doofus came crashing past Mom and Pop and almost barreled Deirdre and Cal over.

"What are you doing here, son?" Pop said, narrowing his eyes.

He looked fine. Healthy. Ornery.

"Mom said some guy was snooping around." He gave Doofus one last scratch behind the ears before straightening.

The dog nosed at Deirdre's hand for more attention.

"You have Deirdre Steen with you."

Very observant. Cal moved his hand to cup her elbow lightly. "Yes, we came from dinner. And the ER. It's been a strange evening."

Mom poked her head out next to Pop, her gray hair curling over her shoulders. "Oh, hi, honey. How was your date?"

Cal and Deirdre glanced at each other. "Um," he said.

Waving her hands, Mom looked past them and into the twilight with a quick frown that morphed into a big smile. "Oh, quit talking out there and come on in. Hi, Deirdre!"

"Hi, Aggie. Bruce," Deirdre said on a laugh as she patted Pop on the arm and entered the house.

After avoiding the wet nose of Doofus while they took off their shoes in the entryway, Cal followed as Deirdre padded in socked feet into the warm living room. Dark brown tail wagging, his parents' retired sled dog trotted over to the living room and curled up on the couch, apparently satisfied that he had completed his mission to greet and lick visitors.

Cal smiled and looked around.

Always the ghosts of his past lived here. This was where he and Elijah had hung out after school. Sometimes Deirdre joined them. Classmates had come over for bonfires on Saturday nights in an open area of hillside below the house.

Memories surfaced of laughing with Elijah and Deirdre and their friends, while Pop pretended to have chores nearby so he could keep an eye on everyone. All while Mom made unending batches of cookies for Cal and his ravenous teen friends. He inhaled, catching the familiar vanilla and warm chocolate scent.

"What's going on, Mom?" he said.

"Want dinner? If you don't mind low-cholesterol cooking," she said too brightly, with a quick glance at Pop, who all but bared his teeth.

Cal paused, uneasy. Mom rarely pulled punches. She would eventually share with him about the person who had come by the house. For now, a whiff of savory venison stew hit him, making his mouth water. "Sure. We had to cut our meal short due to an emergency."

Deirdre nodded with a wry expression.

"You were in the ED? Everything okay?" Mom said.

Cal shook his head. "Can't talk about it. Privacy and all."

"Deirdre, maybe you'll give me the news."

Her blue eyes sparkled. "You know the rules, Aggie. I can't say."

Pop walked over, his gait slightly bow-legged and stiff, like his knees bothered him. It was tough to see him slowing down. Pop settled at the head of the table with a groan and closed one eye to stare at Cal and Deirdre. "No such thing as privacy in this area. Remember how my personal business and all the stuff in the ED went plumb through town and back."

"That's because you told everyone who would listen,

Bruce!" Deirdre said, making Pop sit up straight. "You couldn't stop grumping about the adhesive stuck on your chest from our EKG monitors!"

He pulled a face. "They really should make something that doesn't pull out hair."

"Then we can't monitor your heart." Batting her eyes, she said sweetly, "And *all the stuff* was your heart giving you trouble. Which we fixed. With those EKG monitors that stuck to your chest. Which saved your life."

A master class, Deirdre's handling of Pop.

"*Hmmph.* Still." He rubbed the front of his flannel shirt.

Mom brought over steaming bowls of stew and set them down with a roll of her eyes at Pop. They all ate in contented silence for a minute. The lamp glow and oven-warmed room wrapped around him like a blanket.

Cal set down his spoon. "Mom, your stew is better than I remember. I want this recipe."

Gesturing at him with a piece of bread, she said, "Yes, but it's not the same if it's not made out in the bush in Alaska."

"You guys aren't in the bush." He pointed toward the trees outside the living room windows. "The bush is that way, somewhere between ten miles and five hundred miles away."

"Well, we're not in the town. Or a city. So, we're in the bush," Pop said. "Anyways, I prefer the old recipe."

"The old recipe isn't healthy." Mom's grin bordered on a grimace. It was clear this wasn't the first time they'd had this conversation. "You're welcome that I'm feeding you. Left to your own devices, you'd live on canned franks and beans."

"Well, some of us like franks and beans." Nevertheless, Pop shoveled another spoonful of stew.

Cal knew when the argument wasn't going to go his way. "Hmm."

Pop took a drink of water. "Deirdre, how's your brother and your business?"

"Seems to be going great. The lodge has gotten more reservations as a result of Tuli Sampson's internet posts. Busy is better than the alternative." She paused. "Or did you mean the hospital business? Because that's going well, too. Someone's always getting sick or getting in an accident, it seems."

Pop grunted. Little did he know how outmatched he was verbally sparring with Deirdre. "Seems like everything's coming up roses for you. Thought about settling down?"

Cal whipped his head up.

Deirdre choked on her bite of stew and coughed for a full minute, her face beet red.

Wiping her mouth with the napkin, she said, "That's not … I'm not … I don't have time for that right now."

"What's all this … galivanting with Calvin, then?" Pop pinned her with a steely gaze beneath his bushy brows.

"Galivanting? Pop, come on now," Cal said.

"Bruce, leave the kids alone," Mom interjected at the same time.

Kids? Cal was thirty-six, same as Deirdre.

Drumming her fingers on the table, Deirdre said in a measured tone, "Bruce, we're old friends going out to dinner. Like the most casual of outings."

"That's not what I heard." Pop grunted and dunked his bread into the stew.

Not exactly how Cal saw it, either. On the other hand, they were pretending to date so that they didn't have to endure lines of questioning. Like this one.

He hated threading the needle of truth, but he didn't want to get his parents' hopes up. He'd deal with any confusion later. "What about your text, Mom? It worried me."

"I know a subject change when I see one," she said with a wink, then added, "This man drove up, said he was an assessor from Alaska Department of Natural Resources. Claimed he needed to set up a time to do a survey of the property. Something about documenting mineral rights for a possible claim request. Said a portion of what we think is our property might actually be BLM land, which would open an area for prospectors to seek an exploration and mining claim. I don't understand why they need to resurvey."

He gripped the soup spoon in a tight fist. "And?"

Pop grumbled, "He was real pushy, trying to pick a date to map the property with survey equipment." He barked a laugh. "Our land was surveyed years ago. Pins were set at the boundaries when we purchased the property back then. But that guy didn't want to take no for an answer. Not from your mom or from me." He paused. "Doofus did not like him. That's good enough for me."

A cold chill skittered down his spine. Mom was sweet most of the time, but tough as nails when she needed to be.

If she declined their request, that was that. It irritated him that her wishes hadn't been respected immediately. The timing of the visit wasn't right, either. "What did the guy look like?"

Pop glanced at the ceiling. "Younger fella, maybe thirty, tall and thin. Wore the olive green DNR gear. Flashed ID at us. Looked official."

Damn it. Things were getting out of control. "What did you do?"

Mom gave a smile that came across as mildly aggressive. "After I told him we wouldn't give permission for a survey, your father told him, quote, to 'go to hell' when the man kept on talking."

Pop matched Mom's tight grin. "Then I grabbed my rifle from inside the front door."

Cal's spine went ramrod straight. "That should have taken care of it," he said. Having to defend their homestead by force. Not the situation he wanted them in. Not at all.

"That's what I thought," Mom said.

"I assume he eventually went away."

"Yes, but he seemed pretty determined." Worry creased Mom's forehead as she reached for her shirt pocket. "He left a card." She fished it out of her pants pocket and handed it to him.

Cal didn't recognize the name. The information could be easily verified. Looked official enough. An icy finger of dread worked itself through his chest. "You mind if I hold onto this for a bit?"

"What are you going to do, son?"

"Some research. Does he truly represent DNR? Is the request even legitimate?" He would give the guy a stern warning to stay off his family's homestead. At least at this time. But he held off sharing that part of the plan and instead stowed the card in his vest.

"Who else has property on the Ray Mountain range?" Deirdre asked. "Besides our family's property, yours, and the Koyukon corporation's land?"

Mom shook her head. "We have a lot of acres between the three of us. There are three more property owners with tracts on this range."

Cal looked up. "We were talking about this issue earlier. Could the land speculators actually go around the properties?"

Mom looked at Pop. "That would require making miles of roads to get to the backside of the range. Building bridges strong enough to support large machinery. They'd need to create a work site for all of that equipment as well."

Deirdre toyed with her glass of water. "We should set up a meeting with all of the involved property owners and the corporation elders. Make sure everyone's got a unified front so that we're protected against future incidents. Especially given the persistence of those people, trying to resurvey previously platted land. That's worrisome. Involve town leadership if need be."

"That's a good idea, dear," Mom said.

Pop grunted but nodded.

Pushing up from the table, Mom grabbed chocolate chip cookies from the countertop and passed them around.

Cal's head whirled. He loved Yukon Valley and didn't want outsiders exploiting it for their own gain. Part of him wanted to stand up to those prospectors. Dig in. Fight back.

But his parents couldn't stay here and neither could Cal. Part of his reason for returning to Yukon Valley was his plans to get them moved and settled in a bigger town like Fairbanks, or better yet, Seattle, near Cal. Maybe if there was a sliver of access outside of his family's property, that would resolve the fight with the prospector. Remove the conflict.

Make it easier to encourage his parents to move away.

He took in Deirdre's concerned expression as she chatted with Mom and Pop. Her blue gaze flitted to him, and she shot him a tiny half-smile that warmed him more than the stew.

There might be more to leave in Yukon Valley than the homestead.

Chapter Twelve

D EIRDRE SHOOK OFF the déjà vu from the Garretts's dining room. The glow of lamplight and the warmth from the wood-burning stove in the living room brought back a rush of memories from high school. She and Elijah and Calvin, sitting at this exact table while they plotted their next adventure. Hanging out in the living room while they made homecoming dance decorations. Every recollection, of course, involved Aggie and Bruce.

Truth be told, she now saw in Bruce and Aggie the parents she no longer had. A sigh caught in her chest.

"Well, it's getting late," Aggie murmured.

Bruce grumbled, "No, it's not."

"Yes, it is, dear." She tilted her head toward Calvin and Deirdre.

They thought—oh, no. A sour taste coated her tongue. Deirdre and Calvin's deception looked good on paper, but she never thought through how it could truly affect people she cared about.

"I do have to work tomorrow." Deirdre gave all of them an easy out.

"Want some leftovers to take home?" Aggie said.

"No, I'm good, but thank you."

Bruce pushed back from the table and stood, keeping his hand on the edge for a few seconds too long. "You still coming out tomorrow, son?"

Calvin nodded, but there was weariness in the lines of his shoulders. "I'm planning on it. We'll get the garage repaired and prep for the roofing job later this spring." His voice held a note of resignation she hadn't heard before.

"You still know how to swing a hammer?"

He chuckled. "We're going to find out soon enough, aren't we?"

"Yep," Bruce said. "Well, you two stay out of trouble." Once a father, always a father.

After hugging Bruce and Aggie and exiting the house, Deirdre's heart ached. In the cooler night breeze, she zipped up her coat. Once in the car and buckled in, she turned to Calvin. "Are we sure about this?"

His face was illuminated by the dashboard light. "That's a super vague question with no definitive subject."

"This"—she motioned toward him and patted her sternum—"this fake ... us. Stringing your folks along. Giving hope."

For a split second, he froze like she had slapped him. Then his brows slammed down. "You heard how much they're prying and pushing. If we didn't create a smokescreen, they'd be ten times worse. Never-ending questions. Concerns. Same with Maverick and everyone at work." He put the car into gear and drove away from his parents' home.

"I know. It's just ..."

"Too real?" Calvin's exhale was harsh in the vehicle.

Too close.

A shiver worked through her in response. "Yes."

He rested both hands on the wheel, sinews flexing beneath the skin. "What if we weren't pretending?"

Her stomach clenched. Past and present smashed together in confusing and conflicting ways. If this was real, then she risked losing someone she cared about again. Calvin wasn't staying in Yukon Valley. "I ... don't know. It seems like a bad idea."

He drove back to her place in painful silence. At her house, he parked and jogged around, opening her door and again helping her from the car.

"You don't have to do this," she whispered.

"It needs to look good, right?" The hard edge to his words sent a shiver down her back.

Peeking around, she spied a few neighbors' heads in windows, backlit. Once again, the lie felt wrong. Like she was using him. Lying to everyone.

Lying to herself.

"Let me walk you to the door." His low voice cut through the cold night air. He kept his hand at her elbow, his grip firm but not painful. Just there. Helpful. Available.

She fumbled with the keys until the door opened. "Um."

He leaned down until his breath feathered her cheek. "Appearances, right?"

"R-right."

Tucking one finger under her chin, he tilted her face up. His face only an inch away made her heart stutter.

"Calvin?"

"Is this okay?"

She paused, thousands of thoughts whirling through her mind until they all settled on the man in front of her. "Yes."

His mouth swept over hers once, twice. His lips were steel covered with warm velvet, and he pressed kisses to the corners of her mouth until their breathing became ragged.

Pulling his head up, he rasped, "Tell me to stop and I will walk away."

Her heartbeat stuttered in her chest. So much about this felt right and wrong at the same time. It was a sham but oh so real. "Don't stop," she whispered.

He dipped his head for another breath-stealing kiss that made her head spin.

When he leaned back, she paused and studied him. His face was shadowed in the dim light. Heat poured off of him. His chest rose and fell too quickly, like he'd run a mile.

Her heart hammered in her chest. When was the last time she'd felt this way?

The answer rattled her. *Never.*

Which meant, what? Oh, God, Deirdre wasn't prepared to get in touch with her feelings and address her personal demons. Not tonight. Not after so many years.

"Um, want to come in for a bit? Talk about our plans for later this week?" she managed to say.

With his face in shadow, she couldn't read his expression, but he stood in silence. She sensed him studying her.

"Plans. Sure." Disappointment and a dark intensity laced his words.

She tore her gaze away from his and led him inside, flicking the switch inside the front door to turn on the living room lamp.

The moment the door closed, his arms banded around her.

Chapter Thirteen

CAL HAD TAKEN pretense to a whole new level.

God help him, he liked it. Deirdre's scent. The feel of her soft mouth against his. So many years of wondering what it would be like to have her in his arms like this. She was everything he had never had but deep down always wanted.

But for Elijah.

Elijah. His best friend's memory.

His friend's wife.

Cal didn't care.

Pressing Deirdre against the wall next to the front door, he leaned in, caging her, breathing her in, memorizing the fit of his body against hers. "God, Deirdre." He hauled in a big lungful of air. "This isn't about plans. It's not about me. It's us. We're in this together."

"What do you want?" Her mellow voice unraveled his control.

You. I've always wanted you. Somehow, he stopped the line from exiting his mouth.

Instead, he selected other words. "Another taste. More. Once wasn't enough."

She gave a shaky laugh that rocked his equilibrium. "I'm

on board with that." Gripping his shirt, she pulled, closing the scant distance between them and met his lips.

The tentative brush of flesh against flesh became more insistent. Hotter. Sweeter.

Then another bolt of desire shot through him as he slid his hands up to cup her jaw. He was making up for so many lost years. Everything he had missed was right in front of him. He changed angles, nipping and licking until she opened to him. He swept his tongue between her lips, and she met him thrust for thrust. The air she breathed was the air he breathed. She was a light beckoning him to circle closer. Cal would get burned.

He didn't care.

Cradling her cheek with one hand, he stroked the soft line of her neck with the other. Her sigh sent a red-hot bolt of need straight to his groin. He hardened immediately and needed more.

Trailing his hand up, he laced his fingers through her hair, holding her so he could feast once more, raining kisses over her mouth, her cheeks, her neck. She smelled like flowers and tasted like fresh air and joy. "I can't believe ... this is ..." he said between kisses.

"Calvin"—she wrapped her hands around his neck and drew him closer—"it's been so long."

He kissed her until his head swam. It had been so long.

Too long.

It had been *never*.

This had never happened before.

The concept woke him up as fast as if he'd plunged

through the ice into frigid water. They had never been this close because of her husband. His best friend.

The choice she had made.

The choice Calvin had made not to compete.

Because he couldn't risk being second best.

With a growl of sexual frustration and existential guilt, he rested his forehead against hers and hauled in huge lungfuls of air until he wrestled his body's reactions under control. Deirdre still arched against him with those soft noises that short-circuited his brain. This situation was right, but it wasn't right. After a moment, he gently but firmly tugged her hands from around him and pressed the backs of them to his lips as he stepped back.

Her raw worry and wide-eyed vulnerability almost dropped him to his knees. She licked her parted lips.

Her gaze flickered over him. "Did I do something wrong, Calvin?"

It took him a solid five seconds to form appropriate words in an appropriately gentle tone. "We can't do this."

Rearing back, she said, "This? What? Kissing. We're adults. Pretty sure we can do whatever we want as long as it's consensual." She laughed, then froze. "Unless it's not consensual. Oh my gosh. Calvin. I didn't—"

He lifted his hands. "Oh, no. I am totally on board with everything we were doing. No question about that."

"But?" When he didn't answer, she nodded. "Got it. Hey, strong work on the pretend dating, by the way." The sad mirth in her voice twisted an imaginary dagger in his chest.

Here she was, trying to calm the situation and make him feel better. Always attending to others' feelings, even as he and Deirdre faked their togetherness for public consumption and private relief.

That was the problem. He swallowed a hard lump of disappointment.

This wasn't real.

It could be.

"What if I wasn't pretending?"

She sucked in a gasp. "I ... I don't know. I might—"

At her response, he quickly added, "The question was rhetorical."

"Why?"

They stood way too close to be having this conversation. Even as he took another step back, he said, "Because I'm only here on a temporary basis. This fake relationship is for show."

She paused. "Again, we're adults. We can decide what's right for us." Her gaze met his, momentarily hopeful. Then her gaze slid away.

Cal wouldn't presume to understand everything running through Deirdre's mind right now, but it had to involve a complex set of feelings.

Or maybe it truly was as simple as desire?

He had desire for her in spades, but no way would a brief fling satisfy. It would be like having the first bite of Thanksgiving dinner and then pushing back from the table, stomach still aching with hunger. Then saying *no thanks*. He couldn't do that. Better to stop now and avoid inevitable hurt. "Yes, we are adults. We can agree to do whatever we feel is right."

"But?"

"The other thing. It's still hanging over us."

"What thing?" Her eyes narrowed. Deep down, she knew.

He sure as hell knew. Even if he'd never spoken about it. "I can't ever compare to him, Deirdre."

She stopped moving completely. "No one is comparing you to Elijah."

"I was the second choice. On some level, we both know it."

"Calvin…" Her voice broke. "I don't know what to say to that. It's complicated. Elijah was a special person to both of us. But I never said you were second choice."

"You made a choice, didn't you?"

"Because you left."

Silence stretched between them. The faint sound of a truck engine going through town faded away. Had he missed his chance because of his fear of failure?

"It was obvious that Elijah and you were meant to be together," he said.

"What are you saying?" Her blue eyes went wide, her hand pressed to her neck.

"Was I wrong?"

"Damn it, Calvin." A sob broke free, and she clapped her hand over her mouth.

He wanted to kick himself for ruining their evening. He could still feel the heated imprint of her lips against his.

"This is too much to process. I can't." She half-gasped. "I

can't have this conversation right now. Please."

"Sure, Deirdre. I get it."

"No, you don't. At some point, we need to discuss all of this. Our history." She leaned her head back against the wall and grimaced. "I am not in the right headspace to try to evaluate what I'm thinking and feeling right now."

"You don't have to evaluate anything. I am leaving."

"Like you did years ago?"

"It was the right thing to do then, and it's the right thing now."

Chapter Fourteen

THE NEXT MORNING, Deirdre was up—but not at 'em by any stretch of the imagination. She sipped on her morning coffee and settled into her office chair, not even remotely enthusiastic about a day of hospital meetings and policy development.

Concentrating would be a challenge. Same with staying awake. She had tossed and turned all night, with so many truths she had kept hidden for years, even from herself, tumbling through her brain.

She couldn't betray Elijah's memory. He had been a good partner, even if their early love had quickly mellowed to affection and friendship.

And yet...

With a soft sob, she pressed a hand to her chest, remembering the end.

Stay, Elijah had said a few days before passing away.

He had held out his thin hand for her.

Stay.

The whispered word, the quiet and desperate need for her to be with him in those last moments, burned into her mind.

True to her promise, Deirdre had remained at his side

until he was gone.

For an hour after that, she had sat there, his cooling hand grasped in hers.

Elijah wasn't here anymore. Hadn't been in a long time.

Calvin was here. But not for long.

What did she want?

What had she wanted, those years ago, when everything was possible and both Calvin and Elijah held special places in her young heart? That was the impossible question.

She took a fortifying sip of coffee and dropped her head in her hands, rubbing her forehead with her fingertips.

"Knock, knock, is this a closed meeting?" Mav poked his head in, his big grin dropping to a frown of concern. "You okay, sis?"

"Fine." She motioned to the chair in front of her desk. "Come on in. What can I do for you?"

"Nuh-uh. You're not pulling the administrator crap on your brother." He sprawled in the office chair and rested a booted ankle on the opposite knee. "Spill."

"Since when do you say spill?"

"Since I have an amazing and hip girlfriend who has opened my eyes to the value of sharing."

"I'm fine."

"That's not an answer." He rested his hands on his stomach, ready to stay for a while. "So?"

Deirdre wrapped her hands around the coffee mug, as if the mug was a flotation device that would keep her head above the cold water of the thoughts that dragged at her. "Just busy."

JILLIAN DAVID

"That's also not going to fly. I've seen you busy before. Even doing a million things at once, you're the calmest, steadiest person in the room." He pointed at her. "This is not calm or steady. This is upset. Your eyes are all red."

"Since when did you get in touch with other people's feelings, Mav? You don't even get in touch with your own feelings." Okay, that last bit was harsh, and maybe less true these days. She took another sip of coffee, glaring at it when she didn't immediately perk up. "It's not nice to comment on people's appearances. I didn't sleep well last night."

"Because of?" His light brown eyebrows waggled. "Any juicy news?" He froze, then narrowed his eyes. "Do I need to hurt someone for you?"

She almost laughed. Almost. "Nothing like that." Actually, pretty much like that. Which was the problem. She ground her teeth. "I was thinking a lot."

"Thinking about what?"

"Lots of things."

"Such as?"

"You're being annoying."

He grinned, and for a flash she saw him as her kid brother, circa age thirteen. In the present, though, she wanted to pummel him for getting into her business.

He said, "I can do this all day long, Dee. I got a million more questions I can ask and nothing but time. Shift ended an hour ago."

"Crap."

"Or you can keep talking. It might be good for you."

"Come on, Mav."

He buffed his nails on his medic jacket and somehow relaxed his big frame further into the seat. "Try again."

Where to begin?

She rubbed her forehead. "It's Calvin."

"Before we go any further, do I need to beat him up?"

"What? No!"

Steepling his fingers like the sage he absolutely was not, he nodded gravely, "Yup."

"Yup? What's that supposed to mean?"

"Means I might be a meathead and your brother but have eyes and a brain and can put two and two together. Could you and Calvin be any more obvious?"

"No."

"Um, yes."

"Seriously, there's nothing going on."

"But I can see—"

She huffed. "It's fake."

"Huh?" His jaw hung open.

Leaning on her elbows, she motioned at him. "We're pretending to see each other so that people like you stop bugging us. His folks are driving him up the wall with twenty questions about his future plans. You and everyone in this hospital keep prying into my personal life and setting me up with anyone in the greater Yukon Valley area who's unattached and in my target age group."

"That's like three people." He closed one eye and stared at the ceiling for a second. "Five if you're flexible on gender."

Despite herself, she snorted. "Anyway, it's all a sham."

"Clearly, it's not working."

"What isn't working?"

"Your little plan didn't get me off your back. My interest is way higher now. I'm guessing that Bruce and Aggie are no less invested than before. They'll just bother Calvin with different annoying questions now. But go on with your story." He wiggled his big fingers and lifted his chin, like a target that begged her to pop him *right there*. He sat still, not saying a word. It amazed her how he weaponized silence, but she couldn't deny her little brother.

In the end, Deirdre and Mav were ride or die for each other.

Leaning on one armrest, she said, "So you know how people have been nagging me about my dating life? Calvin's been getting the same treatment from his parents and now from coworkers. We both got tired of it, so we formed a little team to combat the nagging. End of story."

"Denial isn't the same as Denali."

She reared back. "What kind of dumb saying is that?"

He pretended to be offended. "One I made up on the spot."

"It doesn't make sense."

"It does to me. Go on. Tell me more about your relationship, please."

"Mav!" She slapped the desk. "There is no relationship. That's what I'm trying to explain. Calvin and I are old friends and current coworkers, pretending to lightly date so that we get a break from the whisper network."

"Whisper network?" He leaned forward and pinned her with an I-have-a-secret stare. "That sounds illicit and juicy."

"Like you don't know. How did you like it when you had to wait for Lee to decide if she wanted to stay and be with you? And everyone—literally everyone—in EMS, fire, and the hospital were constantly asking you for updates?"

He flicked a frayed area of leather on the armrest. "As I recall, you were one of the people bugging me. Shoe's on the other foot now."

"No." She paused. Okay, yes, she had encouraged her brother to embrace the possibility of a future with Lee while also giving her time to sort out her feelings. The wait was healthy for him. Built character. "My advice was for a good cause. You and Lee are happy together."

"Why is this different?"

"Because whatever people think that Calvin and I have, it isn't real. We're using each other as a cover to survive until after the Breakup Festival and he gets his parents squared away. Then he's going back to Seattle."

Mav cocked his head to the side and propped his chin on his fist. "How do you feel about that?"

She smashed the twinge in her chest and set her jaw against the rush of eyelid-burning emotion. "Perfectly fine. That was the deal."

"Deals can change."

"Not this one."

"What if it could change? If there's a chance for you two? Would you want that?"

She rubbed the prickles of irritation forming on the back of her neck. "It's a moot point."

"If it wasn't a moot point, what would keep you from

trying?"

Another wave of emotions and memories swamped her, and she swallowed a hard lump. "My past is messy. I took a chance on someone and look how it turned out."

"That's a cop-out, sis. You and Elijah had more than ten good years together. Yes, he was gone too soon, and it wasn't enough time. Yes, I miss him. You miss him. We can't bring him back, which sucks."

"I … Elijah, then Mom and Dad. It's been a lot. My heart can only take so much."

"And?"

It took a moment to unclamp her jaw. "I can't go through another loss like that, Mav. Not again."

"There's the truth." His smile was warm but sad.

Understandable as they both missed their parents.

"I've got a lot of baggage to carry."

"The right person can help with the load."

"He's leaving."

"Or not. You don't know for sure." He lifted a hand when she started to speak. "Grief doesn't go away, but you can grow your heart around it to make more room."

She closed one eye and stared at him. Who was this guy and what happened to her little brother? "Oh my gosh, so cheesy. Was that Dr. Phil?"

He shook his head. "Podcast on grief."

"Look at you, working through emotions."

"Yeah, you should try it one day."

"Sure."

"Don't *sure* me, Dee." He pushed to his feet, stepped

around the desk, and leaned down to haul her into a hug around her shoulders that triggered more burning behind her eyelids. Stupid younger brother with a stupid hug being stupid and comforting. "If you won't risk anything, then will you ever truly be alive and whole again?"

"That's deep."

"I want you to be happy."

"Same here."

"I am. Thanks in some part to my meddling sister." He patted her on the shoulder and headed to the door. "You're solid with everything you do, sis. You've got this."

"There's nothing to get."

As he opened the door, he glanced back. "It's scary, but sometimes you've gotta decide that you're worth the risk and take a chance on yourself."

Chapter Fifteen

C AL'S SHIFT ON Thursday had been steady so far. Calm. Pleasant. Bread and butter cases, nothing too exciting, nothing unnecessary. Yukon Valley's patients, in general, were a tough bunch. No cases of hangnails or minor colds came through those ED doors. The people he saw really needed to be in the ED. He felt useful and productive, like he was making a healthy difference in people's lives.

Something he did not seem able to do in any aspect of his personal life.

He paused as he exited the ED. There was a pending item on his to-do list. Holding his breath, he checked his phone for a new message. Nothing. He shook his head and stowed the phone.

Instead of dwelling on things he couldn't fix, he focused on what he could address and followed his nose to the hospital cafeteria. After topping off his coffee mug and filling a lunch tray, he turned, ready to head back to the ED call room.

"Hey, Calvin!"

He paused, spying Dr. Lee Tipton. She was in slacks and a blouse, sitting at a table with Maverick, who wore his usual navy-blue EMS uniform. Their heads were bent toward each other like co-conspirators, which immediately pinged Cal's warning radar. Yet he strolled over. They both glanced at one another then turned to him with twin smiles. Uh-oh. He gritted his teeth.

"How's the shift going, Doc?" Maverick said.

Cal nodded. "Not bad. Both of yours?"

"Not bad." Maverick rapped his knuckles on the wood tabletop.

Lee made a face. "I'm the admitting doc for the hospital, and you're my pipeline of patients. You tell *me* how my shift is going. You've been kind so far." She laughed, brushing a hand over Maverick's on the table. "Don't worry, we won't make you say the q-word."

Quiet. The ubiquitous superstition that every ED physician had. Never say the q-word. Thinking the q-word was even dicey. Allowing that word into your consciousness attracted things like multi-snowmachine pileups or mass moose attacks.

She continued. "Any admits on the horizon? I would like to plan my day."

Cal looked at the ceiling for a second then checked to make sure no one else was in earshot, then de-identified the information. "Maybe a person with pneumonia. I'll see how they do for the next few hours, and if they're still requiring oxygen, we should probably have them stay at least overnight."

"Sounds good." Lee made a face at Maverick. "What? Preempting work duties on call is a karma move. If I ask about admissions now, then I'll either get them done early or they'll be nothingburgers that take five minutes. If I don't ask, then at 6:59 p.m., he's going to dump three unstable critical care admits on me. I know how the universe works. Especially when you and I have seven p.m. dinner plans."

The heated expressions between them made Cal look down at the tray he held. He shifted from foot to foot while they seemed to be telepathically changing their dinner plans to *other* plans.

"Well, I'm going to head back to my ED cave. You two have a good rest of your day."

"Oh, hey," Maverick said with a gleam in his blue eyes, the same color as Deirdre's. "You still planning on attending the Breakup Festival? I think you had been signed up for the dunk for hospice."

He hadn't so much as thought about the Breakup Festival the past several days. Way too much on his mind. "The dunking booth sounds miserable. Yes, I'll be there." He hadn't had any luck getting his shift moved around so that he would have to work that day. Truth be told, he did view participation as a way to honor Elijah by raising money to help other patients and families with end-of-life care.

"It *is* for a good cause." Lee asked, all innocence that Cal in no way bought. "So"—that one word got drawn out into three syllables, thanks to her Southern accent—"are you going to the festival with anyone?"

Cal didn't trust the motives of either one. "Possibly."

"Anyone I know?" he asked.

"Possibly."

"Do tell," she said.

He kept his voice low. "Deirdre and I are attending together."

Maverick and Lee both looked at each other then smiled.

Lee studied Cal until his skin twitched. "It's not a punishment, you know," she said.

"With my sister, it could be." Maverick laughed. He put a hand to the side of his mouth. "She's kind of bossy."

"She's fine," Cal said vaguely. He hated the deception, but giving everyone a controllable bone of gossip to chew on was better than capricious matchmaking and relentless prying.

It was bad enough he had committed to a fake relationship. Earlier this week, he had apparently managed to ruin it. How could someone screw up something that didn't exist? Exhibit A: Cal.

He looked up. The wonder twins were still staring at him.

He patted his phone and pretended to read a text while he juggled the cafeteria tray. "Gotta go. ED needs me."

"Huh," Lee said, lifting an eyebrow.

Chances were, she knew that move. Fake pages worked for years to get him out of boring lunch lectures in residency, timed to occur right after the food was finished and the speaker had begun talking. Busted.

"See ya later, Calvin." She waved.

Before he could turn fully around, they leaned toward each other once again. Low murmurs and laughter chased him out of the cafeteria.

They were two devious peas in a pod.

Two magnets happily pulling toward each other.

Instead of being irritated, Cal felt … empty. Like he was missing out on something.

His life was fine as it was. He had a flexible schedule. Seattle and Washington state had a lot to offer. He could go whitewater paddling or hiking anytime. No obligations to stop him. No coordinating his life with someone else's. Work fulfilled him. His parents might drive him a little crazy at times, but he loved them. Their health and safety was a priority.

He had an entire life in Seattle and a place there. He had friends and colleagues. He patted the phone in his back scrub pocket, knowing that he had a way to fix this entire messy situation.

Sure, things could be better. He glanced back as he exited the cafeteria. Lee and Maverick smiled at each other as they murmured.

That was what he could have. The *better*.

If the situation were different.

If he and Deirdre were different.

He stopped walking. Gripped the tray.

What if she had been right?

What if Cal hadn't ever been second best?

Chapter Sixteen

FRIDAY EVENING, DEIRDRE pulled up in front of the Three Bears. Time for groceries. No dinner with Calvin tonight. An hour ago, he had texted that something had come up.

She knew an excuse when she heard one, but whatever. It wasn't like they were in a real relationship. Could someone be stood up if they weren't actually dating?

She hadn't been looking forward to a dinner out with him anyway. Too many kind but probing questions delivered in his calm, understanding manner would wear her armor away like ice slowly eroding a glacial ravine. Questions she wasn't prepared to answer now, or possibly ever.

Truth be told, she couldn't look at his caring, gray eyes for an hour and not break.

With cooler temperatures in early April, the slush had tightened up once again. She zipped up her coat over her tan sweater and rubbed her gloved hands on her wool pants. As she put her hand on the Subaru doorframe, she glanced at the Yukon Valley Diner next door to Three Bears and froze.

Entering the diner was a man with a familiar tall frame, although he slouched tonight, a winter coat collar pulled up over his neck. Despite the twilight, she could see him in the glass entryway of the diner. Calvin.

He had declined dinner with her tonight.

He was here, at dinnertime, tonight. In the place they were going to have a meal together.

She gripped the handle of the car door, unable to move. Sadness. Irritation. Relief. Betrayal and embarrassment rushed through her, like frigid debris and ice-laden water churning downstream to the ocean. She couldn't filter it fast enough. Couldn't pull that armor around her.

Damn it.

She mentally shook herself. *Deal with it. He had something else to do, and it didn't involve you. Things come up. Or he didn't want to go out tonight.*

There was no actual relationship.

No way was she going to explore why the situation bugged her, beyond the fact that she missed having the halibut special tonight. *You weren't actually dating. There was never anything to get over.*

Deirdre and Calvin knew that, but the other folks in this small town didn't, which was why they had set up tonight's very public dinner to take away the need for friends and family to meddle. The plan was something along the lines of *see all of this dating, folks? Good. Now go bug someone else.*

As she closed the car door to head into the grocery store, a man in slacks and a puffy jacket strode quickly from an SUV into the diner. Something about that man seemed familiar. His jacket strained over a generous midsection, and he ran a hand through his dark hair that was thinning at the temples. When he glanced in her direction, she bent and pretended to search in her pockets for her key.

Who was that guy? She racked her memory.

Then Deirdre froze. The hairs on the back of her neck rose.

No.

No way.

She'd only met him once, in the lodge in early February. She hadn't seen him in a jacket then, but the hairline and stature fit. He sported a light beard now, but the man sure looked like the jerk, Randy, who had tried to sue Deirdre and Mav's lodge into foreclosure so that he could buy it out from under them and exploit the mineral rights on the property. Rubbing her eyes, she looked again, but he had entered the diner.

Couldn't be him. Here? She thought he had run out of town scared after the incident.

What about the guy who stopped by Bruce and Aggie's house and pressured them recently?

What if those two people were connected?

Her blood iced.

Calvin was in the diner shortly after canceling their date. Randy was in there. It had to be a coincidence that they were both in the same place at the same time.

How many coincidences were too many?

Doubt stopped her cold in her tracks. She had to know for certain.

Easing out of the car and closing the door softly behind her—as if someone would specifically hear *her* in the parking lot versus any other patron—she slowly strolled toward the diner. A family of four exited, chattering and juggling to-go boxes as they piled into a vehicle. Once they had pulled out of the parking lot, she slunk toward the nearest window and peeked in. Twilight meant that someone inside might see her. It also meant that she could see inside, though not as clearly as she would have liked.

She squinted. In the back of the diner sat Calvin and Randy in a booth, both visible in profile as they faced each other across the table. They appeared deep in discussion, and Calvin waved off the waitress so that he could continue talking.

Trying not to act like a complete stalker—who was she kidding, she was totally acting like a stalker—Deirdre pulled up her hood over her head and walked past the diner to the gas station, ducked inside, and made small talk with the cashier who, of course, knew her. She bought a few over-priced items and put them in a bag. Exiting after a few more minutes of idle conversation, she once more ambled by the diner.

Calvin and Randy were still there, only Calvin had stood. He stuck out his hand and after a two-second beat, the other man shook it with a curt nod. Calvin's face in profile seemed hard. Clenched.

What was she seeing?

Her mind whirled.

Did it matter? Deirdre had already assumed the worst. Even if Calvin was having an innocent chat with the man who had tried to ruin her family's business and steal their property, the act still seemed pretty underhanded.

Calvin had lied straight to my face so that he could meet with Randy.

She stumbled on a rough patch of slush and rock.

Yet, he hadn't lied. That was the worst part.

Hurrying to reach her car in front of the adjacent grocery store, she fumbled for the keys.

Behind her, a bell clanged against metal. The front door.

Hurry. The keychain snagged on a thread inside of her pocket. Damn it.

"Deirdre?" Calvin's voice reached out to her, ringing clear in the cold air.

Come on, come on. She ripped the keys from her pocket and hit the fob so the car unlocked. Slipping in, she didn't bother with the seat belt as she engaged the engine and backed out, focusing solely on the rearview mirror.

Safety first, right?

If he jogged toward her car, she didn't notice it. Not at all.

As she shifted into drive, she glanced out of the corner of her eye. Calvin's mouth was open, but, with the closed windows, she couldn't hear him. He half-lifted a hand.

She concentrated on the road like it was mission critical.

Petty? Maybe.

Dramatic like a high schooler? Not going to answer that question.

Ignoring another wave of stomach-clenching, adrenaline-powered unhappiness, she pulled onto the state highway and drove the mile or so to her house.

She quickly pulled into the garage and closed the door.

There. Felt safer already. Her stomach growled.

So much for picking up groceries for dinner. Leftovers and gas station snacks would have to do.

She dragged herself into the house and made a sandwich out of cold cuts, sitting at the table and staring blankly at the wall. If the meal had flavor, she couldn't detect it.

Ten minutes later, the sound of a car door closing outside made her lower back tingle. Then came footsteps on the front stairs and pounding on the door that made her drop the rest of the sandwich.

"Deirdre?" Calvin's voice drifted through the wood. To her ear, his tone sounded guilty. "I know you're there."

There was no legitimate reason for him to be here. She had little sympathy for his frustration.

If he felt shame, it wasn't because he had ditched her—it was because he'd been *caught* ditching her. He had met with the enemy, as far as Deirdre was concerned.

More knocking. "Let me in." His words weren't angry. More … pleading.

Hey, he'd stood her up, fair and square. Not like he could spin it in a way that would convince anyone with an ounce of pride. He would have known that she had seen him with the guy who tried to ruin her and Mav.

Not much more to say.

"Please, Deirdre. I can explain."

She couldn't hide forever. As much as she did not want to confirm her feelings and conclusions, at the end of the day she was a fully formed adult who did not back down from uncomfortable conversations. Unless they involved her personal life, apparently.

With a tug to straighten her sweater hem, she lifted her chin and strode to the front door and opened it.

Calvin's chest rose and fell under his black winter coat, like he'd been running. She peeked out. His sedan was parked in front of her house. His face fell into strange shadows with the fading light behind him and lamp light from her house in front of him.

"I want to explain," he bit out.

"There's nothing to explain. You don't owe me anything."

"I think I do."

"Why? You're an adult. You can do what you like. We aren't an item."

He scrubbed at his face. "We kind of are. Or we should be. Or ... damn it." Another big breath moved his coat up and down. "I know that I canceled dinner without giving you an explanation. Then you think you saw me in the restaurant, but I wasn't there standing you up."

"You weren't there? At the diner where we were supposed to eat?"

He leaned a fist against the doorjamb. "Yes. Okay, I was at the diner."

"Then I did see you there. With that guy who tried to hurt my brother and me."

"Yes, but I didn't have dinner. With that guy."

"So, you canceled on dinner, met Randy the asshole at the restaurant instead, and the fact that you didn't consume food is the win in this scenario?"

"Fair." He looked over his shoulder. A neighbor slowly walked their dog past Deirdre's house. "Can I come in for a sec?" He held up his hands. "Please?"

Too emotionally wrung out and too exhausted to argue, she said, "Fine." Then she stepped back.

Chapter Seventeen

C AL DIDN'T KNOW much about women, but he knew
that the word *fine* was secret code for the exact opposite
of *fine*.

This was what it was like for a pirate to walk the plank.
Or a criminal to step up to the chopping block centuries ago.
Menacing music would be the perfect accompaniment to his
morbid thoughts.

He inched into Deirdre's home and shucked his coat and
boots right inside the front door.

"You want something to eat?" she said, one brown eyebrow raised.

"I already ate," he retorted.

Crossing her arms, she said, "Of course you did."

"No, not at the diner. Before going to the diner." In-
wardly, he face-palmed himself. *Good job there setting the
stage for success, slick.*

"You ate before you stood me up?"

"Damn it. That didn't make it better, did it?" After rubbing his damp palms on his pants, he added, "I ate *after*
canceling dinner with you and *before* meeting Randy."
There, all better.

The sadness in her downturned mouth and those angry

glinting eyes nearly knocked his legs out from under him.

"You should have quit while you were ahead," she said.

"I'm getting the impression that there is no ladder tall enough to get out of this hole I'm digging."

"Not in the least." Waving him toward the small living room area, she settled at one end of the couch, drawing her legs under her.

The lamplight and the tan sweater made her skin glow. It did nothing to warm up her icy glare, though.

He held his hands up, as if holding off a charging brown bear. "Let's reset. Deirdre, I am sorry to cancel dinner. I had looked forward to spending time with you."

Her tiny intake of breath tormented him. "It's fine to cancel. We're not dating."

"It's not fine, and we are dating. Sort of."

"Not in a real-world kind of way, Calvin. It's okay. We're not dating. There are no mortgage-bearing complications here. We can make adult decisions and have adult preferences about things like meals." She tapped her lower lip with a finger, making him jealous of the digit. "What hurts more is that you went out with Randy."

"I didn't—"

"I get it. Not a date." One side of her mouth lifted, giving him a glimmer of hope that he might survive this conversation. "That guy was the jerk from our lodge. Why were you talking with him?"

"That's what I wanted to explain." He swallowed, despite a dry tongue. He needed to explain this but keep his plans hidden. While preserving a chance in hell that he could repair whatever fragile relationship was developing with Deirdre. He could walk this fine line. "Randy was behind the guy being at Mom and Pop's house earlier this week."

"How? What?"

Raising a hand, he said, "I needed to figure out what was really going on, so I contacted the man. I, um, acted like an interested party and drew him out so that he would explain his angle."

"Angle? I thought he had left town for good."

"Right after the accident in February, yes. But he and some partners are nosing around again."

"How does that affect us? Mav and I are no longer in foreclosure. Our business is back on track. Randy can't take it away from us. End of story."

Cal shook his head. "Randy's positioning to make a play for other properties along the Ray Mountains. That includes Mom and Pop's property." Which might not be the worst thing ever, even if the execution of his goal and the greater implications chafed at him. "Koyukon corporation land. He's pursuing options and legal loopholes and leveraging finances to try to get access to the ore. He has an eager business partner waiting in the wings. He just needs to extract and supply the minerals. Now."

"He told you that?"

Cal paused to consider his words carefully. He didn't want to lie to Deirdre, but he needed to keep some information locked up tight for now. "Randy is under the impression that I might be the owner of my parents' land. He also believes that I want to sell. He talked too much."

"Why doesn't he quit and go away?"

"He said that this area has a particularly rich deposit of rare earth elements, which has significant demand for science and industry. There's also likely a vein of gold. He's looking at a hell of a revenue stream."

Folding her arms over her chest, she said, "I don't want to give this guy a red cent."

Her fierceness and determination as she sat up straight on the end of the couch triggered a chuckle. "I'm thinking most folks in Yukon Valley agree with you." Cal sobered. "I'm concerned about what lengths he'll go to establish a claim on a parcel. Gain just enough access for a foothold to access the materials. I don't want anyone getting hurt." Especially his parents and Deirdre.

"Chance of him leaving?"

"Basically zero."

"Can we kick him out of town?"

"Not legally. He hasn't committed a crime."

"I'd disagree with that."

"According to law enforcement, you, Maverick, and Lee caught Randy before he could do the crime."

"Who thought being proactive would come back to bite us?" She gave a little sniff.

He rested an arm on the back of the couch, fingers stretching toward her as his torso leaned in her direction, like she was the sun and he an object in space, falling into her gravity. "According to the DNR paperwork in his possession, the Ray Mountain vein particularly in this area has decades of production potential. Could be longer, depending on which mineral is most lucrative at any given time."

A frown pulled her brows together. "So, you weren't plotting with him."

He allowed himself a small celebration that she believed him.

Then he told the truth. "I was making him believe I would work with him. So that I could subvert his playbook." And if his parents were encouraged to move with Cal to Seattle in the process? Mission accomplished. For now, time to push back against her suspicions. "I'm a little hurt that you would think I was consorting with the enemy. Over dinner."

Like a dog with a bone, she wasn't letting up. God, she was beautiful and relentless in her pursuit of the truth.

Narrowing her gaze, she said, "You have mentioned before how you wanted to sell the property and move your folks to a larger city. What's to say you're not setting up their homestead to be the lucrative access point while everyone else holds the line?"

So close. So very close. He reared back, raising his hands. "Hey, now. I might be despicable for other reasons, but I'm not here to sell out Yukon Valley." If altering Yukon Valley ended up happening, he'd feel terrible. But his parents would be safely moved to Seattle and Deirdre and Maverick's property would remain untouched. The people he cared about would be protected.

"Huh. Despicable?" she said with a smirk.

He waited for her to refute the word.

She did not. "So, what's the plan?"

"Uh, what?"

"We should take this information to the local meeting next week. I think we can outmaneuver this guy and leverage those resources for the good of Yukon Valley."

"If that's what everyone wants." He wanted to clamp his mouth shut. Less risk of saying the wrong thing. He tried to recover. "I mean, at least let's make sure everyone is informed and on the same page."

Deirdre worried her lower lip. "That's all very … logical. And thorough. Maybe a little devious, but for a good cause." She paused, then dropped her eyes toward the hands in her lap. "Wow. I might've jumped to a conclusion there. That's not like me."

"Hey, we're all guilty of making assumptions." Had he survived a Deirdre Steen grilling and lived to tell about it?

The scowl on her face suggested that might be the case.

"I should know better. I'm a trained administrator. My job is to gather all pieces of information and sides of the story before reacting." Her beautiful lips turned down at the edges. "Tonight was pure reaction without any data."

A barked laugh erupted. "I want to make a snide remark about the usefulness of healthcare administrators, but this might not be the right time or place."

Her giggle made him hope that things might be okay on the other side of this conversation.

Relief that he didn't have to lie, exactly, unclenched the rigid muscles of his back and shoulders.

He could focus solely on Deirdre now. "Don't beat yourself up. We all deal with events that challenge our beliefs and create doubt." Like everything he thought he believed regarding his feelings about Deirdre. He kept one hand pressed firmly on his knee and the other on the back of the couch cushion instead of wrapped around her shoulders, which was what he wanted. Badly.

"Doubt?" She rolled her lips together, then nodded. "Damn, that's a good observation."

A few seconds passed in thoughtful silence. "Is the issue that you didn't trust me"—he kept his voice neutral—"or that you didn't trust yourself?"

"You're cutting to the bone, aren't you?"

"It's not my intention to hurt." He cleared his throat. He didn't want to push, but it was necessary. "I do feel like we need to clear the air between us. After the other night."

She didn't meet his eyes. "The air is clear. Remember, we're not dating."

The words were out before he could stop them. "What if we wanted to change that?"

The sound of her intake of breath shot into his chest.

Despite the warm lamp glow, her skin paled. "I don't— It's not—"

Leaning forward, he took her hand in his, cradling her fingers. Lightly. She could pull away whenever she wished. "We need to talk about Elijah."

"I don't want to talk about Elijah." The name cracked as she said it.

"It's necessary."

Her eyes widened. The hand he held trembled.

"For what?" she said.

"For us to move forward, separately or together. It's like he's the third person in this relationship. Only he's a ghost."

Her fingers curled around his. "I know. I'm sorry."

"Not your fault. He was a great guy." That was part of the problem.

Deirdre held up her free hand. "You are, too."

"Not like that. Elijah was special."

"You're not wrong. He was loved here in Yukon Valley. Mourned by everyone when he died."

"I know he was special. You picked him."

She pressed her mouth into a line and took a breath.

Finally, she looked up at him, pain and hope and fear all written starkly on her beautiful face. "Calvin, it was complicated," she started out slowly. "I was very happy with Elijah, but our love was more friendship. We had a wonderful friendship, don't get me wrong."

Cal leaned back. This was new information. "But … you loved him? You picked him."

"I can't believe we're having this conversation." She drew another deep breath. "Maybe you're right. We do need to talk about this. It's just painful." He squeezed her hand, and she returned the pressure and gave another wistful smile. "Of course, I loved him. I married him. But people change over time. I wasn't the same person ten years later that I was when we got married."

"You chose him." He was repeating himself now.

Her whisper gutted him. "You exited before I could make a choice."

"What are you saying?"

"Hindsight is twenty-twenty, and I won't look back." A tendon in her neck shifted as she swallowed.

Damn him if he wanted to put his lips on the pulse right there. He forced himself to concentrate on what she was saying.

"I'm saying that I grew to love Elijah, and that love developed into deep friendship and companionship. I also missed you being around. I cared for you, too."

He wanted to ask more, but anguish was etched in the tight lines around her eyes and mouth. He could have altered his own life happiness by taking different action years ago. His fears ... the possibilities were too much to process tonight.

He let go of her hand for a moment. "This, um, arrangement that we have."

"You want to stop."

Cal shook his head. That was the exact opposite of what he wanted, which was the other big problem, for so many reasons. Right now, he wanted to pull her into his arms and kiss her until he couldn't think straight. Hold her so tightly that he couldn't discern the boundaries of his own body or hers. Sink into her softness again and again until they were sated. He'd never have enough of her. His sad laugh surprised him. "Even a pretend relationship with you is worth more to me than a real relationship with anyone else."

Crumbs. Cal's heart would be happy with crumbs if they were from Deirdre.

"I don't understand," she said.

"Are we being completely honest here?"

"I'm scared to." She closed and opened her eyes. "Yes. We're adults. We can be honest."

He picked up her hand and held it to his cheek for a moment. "Deirdre, I'd take a fraction of your kisses and sliver of your time and still consider myself the luckiest guy in the world."

"Calvin, what are you saying?" Her chest rose and fell more quickly.

"It's hard for me to admit this, knowing that the shadow of my friend is always hanging over me."

"I get it. I keep thinking if I have any feeling of attraction, it's a betrayal of Elijah." She laced her fingers with his on the couch cushion. "Then I think about making this— us—real. It's totally unfair of me. You deserve someone whole."

For the second time in as many minutes, he pulled his head back. "That's it. You *are* whole. You're strong and amazing. You're worth someone caring for you. Again. You don't realize it." He shook his head. "Or you don't *want* to realize it." He shrugged. "Hey, I'm an emergency physician, not a psychiatrist." The laugh felt raw but also a relief, like a tense cyst popped. Pressure released. "I'm never going to be Elijah."

The truth, staring him in the face. He'd spoken the words.

She sighed. "Your job isn't to be Elijah."

"I don't know what my job is."

"You mean besides deceiving the entire town so that we don't get pestered?"

"Of course, that." He laughed, the sensation foreign but pleasant. "Actually, I think the gig is up, Deirdre."

The gleam in her eyes warmed him down to his toes. "It was kind of fun having a coconspirator."

Not willing to deal with long-term plans and futures, he took a breath and dove in. "What I'm saying is, I wouldn't mind conspiring with you in a real way."

Her blue eyes locked onto his, and her lips parted.

This moment called for brutal, painful honestly. "You deserve more," he said. Damn it, honesty could be terrifying. "I deserve a chance at more. I think we could be ... that *more* ... for each other."

"Calvin. I ... agree." She shifted and sat up on her knees.

He leaned forward, their lips crashing together. A zing of electricity shot through him right down to his guilt complex. Her taste and the warmth of her body overrode any doubt or rational thought. Every nip of her mouth made him want more. Each breathy sigh added more tinder to the pile. An ember sparked in his belly and ignited a bonfire of desire. He cupped the back of her head, holding her steady so he could deepen the kiss. Her quickening breaths only served to fan the flames into an inferno roaring in his head.

He ran a finger under the neckline of her sweater, the softness of her skin tempting him to explore more. A niggling doubt, in the back of his mind said that he might not be here forever. He had other plans.

Reminded him that he was still second best.

He wanted Deirdre. He had always wanted Deirdre.

Time and distance and denial hadn't eased his desire.

JILLIAN DAVID

Not one bit.

If anything, it had amplified his needs.

Deirdre. He needed the strong, smart woman sitting in front of him with a flush painting her cheeks and her lips temptingly parted. He wanted to hear more of those moans. He wanted the chance to have her as a coconspirator in the future.

How much future, he wasn't prepared to assess.

He leaned in to meet her in another breath-stealing kiss that gave him vertigo. He was acting like a randy twenty-something instead of a fully formed and functional adult.

Pulling back for a second, he murmured, "This feels amazing. Are you okay?" He wasn't asking only about the physical but the emotional as well.

Taking a shaky breath, she smoothed his shirt fabric that had crinkled under her fisted grasp. Her tongue darted to lick her lower lip, that small move sending shock waves of need to his groin.

"Very okay." She moved forward, and he eased himself back on the couch, drawing her down with him.

Her face, her scent, her softness filled his senses. If Deirdre was a drug, he was hooked.

Skimming his hands under the sweater, he stroked over her back and down her sides. Gone was the high school girl he had fallen for. In her place was a woman with curves that tempted him to touch more. Time had changed her, inside and out. Time had changed Cal, too. He rested his hands at her waist, shaking with the craving to grip her soft skin. To rip off the clothes between them.

154

After all of these years, had they missed their opportunity for time together? It wasn't too late. He refused to think of anything involving the logistics of a future. He shifted his hips to relieve the pressure from his rising erection.

He wanted more than a fling. God, he wanted Deirdre.

He lifted the bottom of the sweater, exposing even more skin and making his mouth water in anticipation of tasting. "Are we still good?" His voice sounded like gravel.

A smile crossed her face like the first sunrise after a long winter. She maintained eye contact with him right up until the point when she flipped the sweater off and tossed it on the floor. "Very good." She pressed her palms to his chest and leaned forward, brushing her bra covered breasts against him.

He loved the connection, but by God, they both had way too many clothes on. She undid the first two buttons of his shirt, her warm fingers sending more sensual electricity through him with the quick, light movements that scrambled his brain.

Through the entirety of his life, he had never met a woman like Deirdre and never would again. Tonight was because he and Deirdre had chosen each other.

He palmed her breast through the bra, his desire spiking another ten notches. He drifted his thumbs over her nipples, appreciating the hard peaks that rose after only a few strokes. He rolled his lips inward, wanting to taste and tease her breasts.

"Calvin." She lay down on him for another scorching kiss.

Minutes later, they pulled away, panting.

Second best felt like first place right about now.

"Not here." He sat up, holding Deirdre by her hips.

"What?" Her confident gaze wavered.

"I want this to be perfect. We are not making out on the couch like a couple of high school students."

"It seems like that's exactly what we were doing." Her grin lit up her face and made her glow.

"We need to move to a location where I can touch every inch of you, and we don't risk throwing out our necks or backs. The bed?"

"No guarantees we won't throw something out there, either." She twined her arms around his neck, pressed against his chest and kissed him until his arms inched farther around her back. He couldn't get close enough. "Yes. The bed."

Chapter Eighteen

DEIRDRE STARED INTO gunmetal gray eyes that burned into her. Contingency logistics and overanalyzing the fun out of any given task were her superpowers, but for once in her life, she simply wanted to experience her feelings. Not be in charge of what-ifs and plans A, B, and C. She didn't want to dissect her emotions until nothing of substance remained.

She knew Calvin. She trusted Calvin. Being with him would change everything. Was she ready for that?

Yes. She wrapped her arms around his neck and kissed him until her head spun.

He pushed up from the couch, gripping her hips as he walked toward the bedroom, carrying her. A thrill zipped through her nerve endings, leaving delicious tingles in its wake. When was the last time she had felt like this? She locked her ankles behind his back and pressed her lips against the hammering pulse on his neck.

Never. She had never felt quite like this, and on some level, it scared her.

On some level it freed her.

Deirdre reveled in the flex of his back and neck muscles under her hands as he held her securely and strode to the bedroom.

What about her past? Her future?

She focused on the man she had known for so many years but who seemed brand new.

It was time to attend to the present.

He bumped his knees against the bed and deposited her on the mattress with a gentle stomach-flipping drop. "Last chance to bail before I lick every inch of your body." His words might have sounded light, but his direct gaze was intense, and his shoulders were tense. He was dead serious.

Deirdre desperately wanted to feel *something* again. Something good. Something for herself.

She wanted more than a fake relationship. She wanted to push past fear, doubt, and the regrets of time.

She wanted Calvin.

Everything would change.

It already had changed when they kissed a week ago.

"Who says you're the one doing the licking?" She sat up and untucked the shirt from his waistband.

His eyes darkened. "I don't want to rush this, Deirdre. We've got all night. I intend to use my time wisely."

"Who's rushing? Get naked."

"As an administrator, you might be used to ordering people around, but I've taken AIDET training. I'm now an expert in customer experience." His chuckle rumbled through her ribs.

His presence was so attractive, she literally could feel her nipples tightening. So sexy. She stopped moving. Wait, what? "You actually watched *and* remembered the staff training modules about patient communication?"

He pulled off his shirt, revealing a lean torso with a light dusting of dark hair that arrowed downward. The view turned the inside of her mouth to sand.

"Communication and satisfaction is important, is it not?" he asked with a grin.

Finally, she unstuck her tongue. "I can't believe we are talking about AIDET, now. Here." She gasped as he trailed his fingers over her shoulders and down her arms to rest on her hands. The light connection made her crave more of her body touching his.

A wicked glint in his eye as he lifted his chin preceded his challenge. "You know what? Let's see if the boss can recite the five AIDET steps to the student."

"Huh. Easy." She took a breath.

"Not yet. Do it while I'm kissing you." He unclasped her bra and pulled it away, then knelt over her, his breath warming her skin.

Never in a million years would she have used a customer service tool as foreplay, but here she was, trying to remember the steps that all staff had to learn ... as Calvin drew tantalizing, feather-light patterns over her neck and upper chest.

"AIDET? You sure?" she asked.

He shot her a wolfish grin. "How else can we confirm that I paid attention?"

"I think you're paying lots of attention right now."

"Mmm." He nipped the skin over her collarbone until she shivered.

"AIDET. A. Acknowledge."

"Ah." He traced the underside of her breasts with his finger. "Good evening, Ms. Steen."

"This is strange, Calvin."

He stopped. "No. This is kind of fun, for once in our lives." He kept his palms on the fullness of her breasts and lightly stroked both nipples with his thumbs until she squirmed. "Continue. There may be incentives if you pass the module."

"Ha." Her shaky laugh slid into a sigh as her tips tightened under his touch. An ache formed deep in her pelvis. She cleared her throat. "AIDET. Acknowledge. Next one is I. Introduce."

"Introduce. Correct. Ahem." His expression became professionally pleasant. "Hello, my name is Calvin, and I will be doing my best to make your toes curl this evening." He licked both thumbs and rubbed them over her nipples. Then he blew across her damp skin.

Her heated insides warring with the cool, wet skin made her legs shift restlessly, arching toward him for more. He paused his movements when she couldn't form words. "Go on. What's the next one?"

"D. Duration of service."

"Duration?" He pursed his lips and pressed a kiss to the underside of one breast, then the other. "It is going to take a long time to slowly get you worked up and hot for me. Multiple times. I'm providing this information so you may plan for your evening."

She gritted out words. "This whole situation is an EEO

complaint waiting to happen."

His teeth gleamed white in the lower light. "That's funny." He dipped his head and sucked one nipple into his mouth, brushing the tip with his tongue. All the while he eased his other hand lower down her abdomen. When he reached her waistband, he slid his fingers underneath and lower, stopping right above her throbbing core.

"Calvin?" She gasped, bucking beneath him, trying to bring her heated flesh into contact with his hand, but he kept his fingers an inch away from relief.

"Continue," he said, eyes dark.

"Oh my gosh, you're terrible."

He grazed the hood of her clitoris with one finger, and she moaned.

"AIDET," she burst out. "Fine. E is Explanation."

Releasing one breast with a final lick that made her shudder, he peered up at her with an owlish expression. "Explanation. Ms. Steen, I intend to completely satisfy you. To accomplish this, I will use my mouth and fingers and … so much more."

He grazed her sensitive clitoris with a fingertip, and she hissed and arched toward his hand. Waiting until he received her nodded assent, he slid off her leggings and underwear.

His pants brushed against her legs, the friction of rough fabric against soft skin sparking along her nerve endings. "Oh, Calvin."

Kissing the skin over her hipbone and upper thigh, he growled and lightly nipped. Palming her thighs, he pressed her legs apart.

Then he paused, his breath fanning sensitive flesh. "You're not finished yet," he said.

Drolly, she replied. "You have no idea."

Shaking his head, he smiled. "With the last part of AIDET, you get a reward."

"Pizza party? Points toward a corporate-branded satchel?"

"Way better." He dropped a kiss right on the juncture of her thigh and abdomen, inches from where she burned for his touch.

She tried to lift her hips toward him, but he held her in place and kissed her again, a tiny bit closer to heaven. But he didn't move his mouth from that spot.

Heart pounding, she forced herself to think. Her brain wouldn't cooperate. When he paused, she groaned in frustration.

"AIDET," she blurted out. "T. Thanking. Last one is thanking the customer."

Without warning, he swept his mouth over her labia, and she made a high-pitched keening sound. Then he pressed the flat of his tongue against the sensitive seam.

Lifting his head once again, he said, "Ms. Steen, thank you for this amazing opportunity to serve you today. You may receive a phone call regarding your care. I hope you will be able to rank my service with a high satisfaction score."

The laugh that bubbled up from deep inside morphed into a guttural sigh as he returned to his work, licking and nipping at her heated flesh. He gripped under her hips and raised her toward him, making satisfied growls as he drove her need higher and higher.

She was flying. "Calvin, I want you—" She reached toward him.

He planted her hand on the comforter and patted it to stay there. "Not yet. Soon." He panted, his breath hot against her already heated skin. Nudging her legs farther apart, he lifted his head, first looking down at her, then met her eyes. "My God, this is amazing."

"I'll say."

He grinned again, this time tracing a finger between her folds.

A gurgle and a hip wiggle was all she could manage.

He eased his finger into her. "You're so wet."

No shame. This was Calvin. This was Calvin in a whole new light. Actually, it was the same light, only now she acted on her feelings. "How could I not be wet, given everything you're doing to me? This is because of you."

He started to stroke inside of her, eventually adding another finger. "It's you, Deirdre. You're amazing."

The delicious stretch primed her desire, like a heavy snowpack hanging at the top of the steep mountain. "Please." She gasped.

"I've got you." Dipping his head, he flicked his tongue over her clitoris as he curled his fingers with each thrust.

Tension spiraled, chasing completion. "I'm ... oh God, Calvin." When he gently sucked on her nub and pressed his fingers deeply, the avalanche of sensations broke free in a quivering, shaking full-body response that seemed to roll on and on.

He continued to move his hand and drew out the orgasm

through several delicious aftershocks until she finally came to rest in his arms.

His half-mast gaze met hers, and he growled contentedly.

Boneless, she lifted her head, peering at him where he lay with his cheek against her open thigh. "Time for some customer service feedback."

Chapter Nineteen

"OH?" HE SAT up, muscles quivering and tense. It felt like he'd run a marathon, his heart pounded so hard in his chest. Air burned as it sawed in and out of his lungs. But he could easily go an extra mile. Cal wanted nothing more than to plunge into her, over and over, as they lost themselves in sexy oblivion.

She followed his movement and also sat up. Then she unbuttoned his pants and motioned for him to stand so she could push the garment over his hard erection standing at the ready. She touched him, and he nearly exploded on the spot.

"Damn it. Later," he gritted out.

"You want me to AIDET you?"

"Hell no. I can barely form words. I want you. So much." He bent down to the floor and fished in a pocket, pulling out a condom packet.

With an eyebrow waggle and a bite of her lip, she said, "Let me." Lightly, she pressed on his chest until he fell back on the bed. He didn't believe her innocent act for a second, based on the feral glint in her blue eyes. He fisted the comforter, trying not to grab her. Giving her this time to play.

And play she did. Deirdre slid the condom over his length, so slowly that his eyes rolled back in his head as he saw the northern lights. Then she cupped him until he spread his legs wider. Each stroke over his sac triggered a spine-deep shudder as his testicles drew up, tense and ready. He fought with everything he had to let her be in control.

Deirdre knew what she wanted, and he loved that about her. Loved this whole scene. Their skin against each other, the trust, the mutual care.

She paused.

"Deirdre, you okay?"

"Yes. Are you okay if I, um—" She made a jumping motion with her hand.

Right this minute, he was no genius, but he could put two and two together. "You want to giddyap?"

Her cheeks turned a lovely shade of pink. "Well, yes. If you're okay with it."

"That might be one of my favorite fantasies. You. On me." His penis moved in time with his pulse.

He had no shame. It was obvious how much she turned him on, and he wanted her to know it. She was stunning, all confidence, soft curves, and glowing skin.

Scooting up into the middle of the bed, he reached for her, guiding her to kneel over his erection. The brush of her heated flesh over his penis tip cracked his restraint, and he clutched her thighs until she yelped.

Somehow, he loosened his grip. "This is going to feel amazing," he said, voice hoarse. "If I survive it."

Slowly, she lowered herself onto him. With every torturous inch, they panted in unison.

"Oh my God." She gasped when he bottomed out in her.

They breathed together. Then she gently rocked against him.

He pulled her down harder. "Deirdre." Pressing a thumb against her clitoris, he kept time there as he met her movements with upward thrusts of his own. The heat from her palms against his chest would be imprinted there forever.

After a few minutes, she slowed her pace.

He rolled them over, hooking her knee over his shoulder and driving himself in more deeply. Thrusting faster, he clamped his jaw tight when her inner muscles fluttered around him. Sweat rolled down his temple as he held off on his own release, wanting her to chase her own first.

In a burst of high-pitched cries and gasps, Deirdre climaxed, her inner muscles pulling him in even deeper. Then with a roar, he followed her over the precipice, her body milking him dry until they both collapsed limp on the bed, panting.

He kept his full weight off of her but nestled his face into the crook of her neck, licking at the salty sheen of sweat on her skin. She tasted like comfort and completion.

After cleaning up and returning to bed, Cal lay on his side and tugged Deirdre so that her back rested against his chest. He wrapped an arm around her and reveled in the rise and fall of their breathing in unison. With his hand pressed against her sternum, he counted heartbeats.

"That was amazing," she murmured, somehow managing to snuggle even closer to him.

His body fit perfectly with hers. A blast of conflicting emotions ran through him, none of which he wanted to deal with at this time. "You're beautiful. Incredible." He inhaled the floral scent on her hair and the warm musk of their passion clinging to their heated bodies.

That was the problem, wasn't it? She was a special woman. She was his best friend's widow. She deserved more than a guy who didn't plan to stick around Yukon Valley.

"Are you okay?" she asked, half turning in his arms.

He loosened his clenched embrace. No way would he tell her about his inner conflict. He would rather hurt himself than take anything away from her pleasure tonight. "Absolutely." He kissed her shoulder. "I don't have words for what we experienced."

"Me neither. Except, we should do that again sometime."

He smiled. "Agreed. But—"

"But?"

"Someone of my advanced age needs recovery time."

She snorted. "You're the same age I am."

"I would never call you old."

"As long as you call me."

He chuckled, but his laugh tasted bittersweet. "Will do. Mm-hmm." He pressed his lips against her neck until she gasped and writhed once again.

They tumbled back into pleasure together for a second time.

THE EARLY LIGHT gave the room a bluish glow. No sound came from outside of Deirdre's house. Cal smiled as he glanced around the bedroom, then stopped when he spied the dresser.

On it sat a picture of Elijah and Deirdre, smiling and faces together. Healthy and happy. Youthful. From a time before Elijah had become sick.

Taking a solid breath required more effort than Cal was capable of.

So did analyzing the layers of feelings the past twelve hours had churned up. He'd rather focus on the here and now.

At some point in the night, Deirdre had turned to face him. Those kiss-swollen lips, now relaxed and calm in sleep, had been open in pleasure last night. Several times. What he'd give to see that expression again and again. What he'd give never to leave the crystalline perfection of this exact moment. Right here.

"Morning." Deirdre stretched in his arms, catlike, purring when their chests rubbed together.

That simple and sexy movement triggered his penis from relaxed to ready in a split second. *Down, buddy.*

He held onto control as he dropped a kiss onto her forehead. "Good morning."

She gave him shy half-smile. "I suppose our pretend relationship isn't so fake anymore."

"Um, yeah."

Trailing her fingers over his pectorals, she said in a soft, sleep-roughened voice that triggered a hungry response deep inside of him, "I loved everything about last night."

He brushed a thumb over her soft cheek. There was a pause, then he said, "I did, too."

She pulled back, her hair tangling between her head and the pillow. "But?"

God, she was way too observant. "We may have painted ourselves into a bit of an emotional corner."

Her eyes narrowed. "Go on."

"Look, what we had, here, last night. There aren't words strong enough. Wonderful. Sexy. Addicting." The words spilled out. "But you deserve more than I have to give, Deirdre. You deserve a solid future. We took our pretend relationship and ran with it. Literally." He stroked her shoulder. "We changed our rules."

Lines formed between her brows. "No one needs to know that things changed."

"My car was parked on the street all night. It's a small town. Cat's out of the proverbial bag." He swallowed. "Besides, you're the kind of person who deserves a long-term, real relationship."

"You think you know what kind of person I am in this respect?" Her eyes narrowed. Her chin lifted.

Loaded question. "You're a quality person who should have someone solid to stick around. Not a one-night stand."

"First of all, I can have a one-night stand if I want one."

"You're right."

"Also, no one's asking for anything long-term."

"Aren't you? Deep down." Cal's world back in Seattle didn't include Deirdre, but on the other hand he couldn't visualize a world without Deirdre in it.

"Don't presume to know my thoughts. What I want." Her weary sigh sent his stomach into a spiral. "My dreams."

Oh crap. "That's not—"

"Look, Calvin, if you're having regrets, that's fine. But you need to own your reaction."

"I own it, but not—"

The regret on her face as that sad smile fell hit him like a two by four.

"I never asked you for anything," she said quietly. Too calmly.

"Except faking a relationship. Which, full disclosure, I agreed to as well." He nodded. "We'll keep up the pretense until I'm gone. I won't renege on that promise."

"If that's what you want to do, then fine." *Fine.* Her tone suggested it was anything but fine.

"I will finish our deal," he said. "Shield both of us from friendly fire. Aim the gossip elsewhere." Like he did last night? Hell of an aim. Sleeping with her had not been part of their plan.

She opened then closed her mouth, blotches of red blooming on her neck and cheeks. "I think you might want to head on out. You probably have a busy day." Her words might be polite and terrifyingly calm, but he read the clamped jaw and tight lines around her eyes.

"Deirdre, I'm sorry."

"Sorry for last night?"

"No. Never." *I'm sorry I can't be the future you need and deserve.* Even now, he couldn't speak the words aloud.

"Then we're good." Her lips pressed together. "Do you need me to get the front door, or are you okay closing it behind you?"

Chapter Twenty

LATER THAT MORNING, Deirdre scratched behind the ears of retired sled dog Kenai until the dog left happy drool marks on her fleece-lined outdoor pants. Kenai trailed along, tail wagging, as Deirdre fed the rest of the babies. Mav had an EMS shift, and of course she had run late this morning because, hello, sex with Calvin. So, she and her brother hurried to get breakfast out for hungry guests and never-been-fed dogs.

Thankfully, the guests wanted to sleep in, so she had time to prepare their meal.

"Still want to take them on their walk?" Mav placed a bowl in front of Denali, who shook her long, luxurious tan fur. With daytime temperatures rising, the Malamute had started to shed. They'd be able to spin yarn and knit a sweater out of the amount of fur she would drop in the next few months.

She unzipped her own jacket to allow cool air to flow across her fleece pullover underneath. Even growing up in Alaska, she sometimes struggled to get the right clothing-versus-weather combo.

"Planning on it. As soon as the guests are done with breakfast. I was going to take this crew for a trot around the meadow." She lifted her chin toward the snowy expanse that stretched between the stand of trees protecting the lodge and the hills rising in the distance.

"Watch out for Kaaktuq. He's been especially flatulent lately. God knows what he's been eating besides kibble."

On instinct, she set the bowl down and stepped back quickly. Kaaktuq had only eyes for the food and shoved his head in, snorting while he ate. His big fluffy tail collected slush as it whipped wildly in happiness.

"Got it." She put another food bowl down for Bob, who gave a lopsided doggy smile before digging in. "Meadow trails still holding up?"

"A little muddy, but they'll be okay."

She pointed. "Brought my mud boots."

"Yeah, you'll be fine, then." He reached down to pat Bob on his irregular-looking head attached to his irregular-looking body. "These guys will love the sloppy terrain."

"I'll love cleaning them up afterward."

"Yep." Mav pulled apart a bale and replaced old hay with new in each kennel. "Anything else you need before I get out of here?"

"No, I'm good."

He paused, his eyes inscrutable behind his sunglasses. "Sure about that?"

"Of course."

He grunted. "Anything you want to *tell* me?"

For the love of prying younger brothers.

She huffed, "Nope." No way was she sharing details about her personal life with Mav.

"Because Hilda texted. Something about a car parked in front of your house last night."

Deirdre's face heated, despite the cool air. "Sometimes I hate that this is a small town. That's none of Hilda's business." Her so-called friend and local paramedic was checking up on her. Neighborly, but invasive.

Crunching melting snow with a boot, he put his gloved hands on his hips. "I mean. It wouldn't be the worst thing, having a car parked outside your house last night."

Deirdre inhaled the scent of fresh hay and clean cool air. The beginning of April and it was in the low forties. Nearly T-shirt weather for the interior of Alaska. Which meant in a few months trails would be open for summer hiking, and in a matter of days or weeks rivers and lakes would unfreeze.

Breakup Festival was right around the corner. Deirdre shook her head. Seriously, what had she been thinking, pretending to date Calvin, hoping that no one would pay any attention. Believing that fake-dating him would provide her some social armor. A reprieve from the prying.

Heck, her heart was so bruised from Elijah leaving her, she couldn't manage even a fake relationship.

But Calvin's lips, his hands, his ... everything. Last night had been more magical than anything she'd ever had with Elijah, and the fact that she made a comparison made her sick to her stomach.

"It doesn't feel right or normal," she said. "After ... Elijah and all."

A small voice inside reminded her that after the wedding, she and Elijah's relationship had quickly grown into more of a friendship. Less sex, more companionship. It worked for both of them. If she missed the physical connection with him, his support and kindness more than made up for it.

Now, she had a glimpse of support and kindness *and* physical attraction. Instead of grabbing the opportunity with both hands, she hesitated.

It wasn't a contest. They were two completely different people. She was a different person now than she was even five years ago when Elijah died. A far different person than she was multiple years ago when she and Elijah had gotten married.

"It might never feel normal, sis. Pretty sure that's okay."

Thank God for sunglasses hiding her burning eyes. "It doesn't matter. Calvin left early this morning."

"Why?"

"Why what?"

He crossed his jacket-clad arms with a shush of insulated material. "Did he leave on his own, or did you send him out the door?"

"It doesn't matter."

"Of course it matters. You matter. You and Calvin matter, if that's what you want."

"He left. End of story."

"So." He pulled his sunglasses down his nose and squinted at her. "You freaked out and kicked him out." He paused and pushed the sunglasses back into place with a smug expression. "I'm probably leaving out a lot of juicy details, but that's the gist of it, huh?"

A hand on her hip, she said, "Aren't you late for work?"

"Look"—he extended his hands—"maybe you won't give yourself permission to find love again, so I'm going to give you permission." He glanced down at fawning Kenai, pressed next to his leg, then back to Deirdre. "Go on, sis. Have fun. Live a life. You and Calvin can be good together."

"He left me," she blurted. "Elijah." She stammered. "Elijah left me. Dammit, I'm tired of being left. It hurt. I'm scared of being left again." Even worse. Elijah had asked her to stay, and then he had left.

"Aw, Dee." He pulled her into a semi-awkward hug that only a younger brother could give. "Listen, you'll figure this all out. I know you will. If you want any advice, I'm here."

She stepped back, took off her sunglasses, and swiped at the tears on her cheeks. Popping the eyewear back on, she said with forced levity, "Get to work, Mav!" She swatted at his arm covered by the coat material. "No way am I taking relationship advice from my little brother!"

He laughed as they hurried back toward the house. "You know I'm right!"

No. She didn't know that.

What Deirdre knew with 100 percent certainty was that her heart couldn't take any more pain. The harder she loved, the harder it hurt when people went away.

They always went away.

Her parents had left her in that awful crash on the river.

Elijah had left her.

Calvin had left her.

Didn't matter the details. The fact that it had happened was enough for her to recognize the pattern and close the door. No risk meant no pain, which was incentive enough.

She paused while Kenai caught up with Mav as they walked back to the house.

Damned Breakup Festival. Damned fake relationship. Damned small town.

Her phone dinged. Text from Calvin. Her heart skidded in her chest.

"*Meeting with elders and mayor's council this Tuesday night 7 p.m. at the town hall.*"

No mention of last night. No mention of their next fake date. Nothing.

At some point, they'd need a game plan for the Breakup Festival. Or not. Maybe they should let the farce of a relationship die where it lay.

She texted back a cordial, "*Sounds good, thanks*" that she in no way felt.

Guess their next date was a meeting.

Chapter Twenty-One

CAL PAUSED WITH his hand on the front door handle of Mom and Pop's house Saturday evening. After looking around to ensure the homestead appeared safe, he pasted on what he hoped was a neutral expression, similar to when he had alarming results to convey but didn't want to worry the patient.

He sucked in a breath. Let it out. Smoothed his palm over his fleece jacket and black pants.

Opened the door—anything to stop the relentless yapping going on behind the entryway.

Doofus greeted him exuberantly with the usual sniffs and wet-nose nudges, demanding ear scratches. Cal dutifully obliged by petting his parents' beloved mutt.

The aroma of pot roast and carrots drew him deeper into the cabin. He was surrounded by wood and warmth and childhood memories that ended right when he left Yukon Valley.

Dodging a doggy lick to the cheek, he sat and took off his boots, setting them inside the entryway. Then he hung up his fleece jacket. In socked feet he entered the living room.

"How's it going?" Pop said, from where he relaxed in his

ubiquitous recliner position. beer frothed in a glass on the table next to him.

"Good." Cal lifted his chin. "That stuff safe to mix with your blood thinners?"

Mom made a *hmmph* noise, drawing Cal's attention. Then she rolled her eyes and turned back around to meal prep.

Pop glared at him. "You ever stop being a doctor? Getting in people's business?"

"You're welcome?" He ran his hand over his hair. "Twelve years of education and you still won't listen to my advice."

"Medical advice is just that—advice." Lifting the glass, Pop added, "It's alcohol-free."

Knock him over with a pine needle. "No way."

He gestured. "Have some." Pop peeked over his shoulder and lowered his voice. "It's terrible."

Cal laughed. "I'm impressed. Old dogs *can* learn new tricks."

"See? I changed my ways."

He leaned down as if scrutinizing the man in the chair, then called out, "Mom, what did you do with Pop? This guy is an impostor."

Dishware clinked in the sink as Mom said, "Don't get too excited. We're shopping in Fairbanks this week. We have to make it past the package store, the smoked meats shop, and a bakery."

"Hey, Aggie. Some people have superior mental ability to resist temptation."

"Oh, you've got ability, all right." She set a plate down especially hard.

"Quit picking. All this stress isn't good for my agita."

"With respect to your Italian ancestry, you don't have agita." She rubbed a strand of hair off her forehead. "You have a heart that was overdue for a sixty-thousand-mile tune-up when the warranty ran out."

"Huh. How's dinner coming along? I'm starving."

Cal shook his head at Pop's subject change. Avoidance, thy name was Pop.

However, the old man remained planted in the recliner. It wasn't that Pop was lazy or un-helpful. He'd be in the kitchen helping out if Mom would allow it. The last time she let him run amok with food prep, he scorched one pan and almost lit the wood walls of the house on fire, in his pursuit of creating bacon wrapped venison. Cal felt an imaginary twinge of his coronary arteries clogging up, at the mere thought of the greasy food.

Mom said, "You two come on over. It's ready. Say, where's Deirdre?" Mom was also an expert on the topic switch. "I thought she'd be coming by with you tonight."

For this conversation, Cal would need a real alcoholic beverage. He pushed up from the couch while Pop did the same from the easy chair, their twin grunts foreshadowing Cal's post-retirement future.

Transporting a large dish from the kitchen to the pad on the table, Cal said, "She had things to do that didn't involve me."

"Huh. That's surprising. You two have been thicker than

thieves lately," Pop said.

"Something like that," Cal mumbled.

"Anything wrong?" Mom sat down first, and Pop and Cal followed.

"No." He ignored the assessing stares of his parents. "Wow, that looks delicious, Mom. Mind if I serve up?" One good subject change deserved another. And another.

They passed plates then dug in for a few minutes. Mom's pot roast was legendary. He groaned as the flavors hit his tongue. "This is really good," he said after several bites.

"It's not the same," Pop groused.

Mom glared at him until he lowered his head and continued eating. In silence.

With a bland expression, she tilted her head toward Cal in explanation. "Less salt, lower fat. Your father isn't a fan."

Cal shrugged and stabbed a carrot. "You know what my favorite food is?"

"What?" Mom said.

"Anything I didn't have to cook!" He popped the bite in and chewed, giving Pop a pointed smile.

Another grunt that sounded almost like agreement. "So, are you sticking around until the Breakup Festival?" Pop asked.

"The committee won't let me out of the hospice dunking booth assignment, so I guess that's the plan. My work contract goes through the end of this month." He tore off a piece of sourdough bread and chewed. "So, any thoughts to what we'd discussed? Wrapping things up in Yukon Valley. Moving to someplace bigger. I worry about the resources here for you two."

After swallowing a mouthful of stacked carrots that he clearly did not hate, Pop shook his head. "This is home, son. We've decided to age in place."

"Okay, I know *aging in place* is the new thing touted by AARP. But aging in place implies there are resources that support you in your golden years."

"I'm not decrepit!" Pop said.

Mom lifted her hand. "Honey, that's nice that you want to help. We wouldn't know what to do in an unfamiliar big city. We have doctors here and we have friends—all in Yukon Valley. We don't want to leave our home."

Yes, but Cal had a life away from Yukon Valley, and it seemed unfair that he had to bear responsibility to help his folks as they got older. "What is your Plan B, then?"

"No Plan B," Pop said. "Why do we need one?"

He resisted the urge to drop his forehead in his palm. "Because at some point you won't be able to swing an axe or shovel snow off the roof. This place was a lot to keep up when you were young. It's not getting easier. You may need more help."

"We're tough, right, Aggie?"

"Some of us more than others," she said dryly.

"I'm not going to be around to help, you know," Cal said.

"We do have other friends," Mom said.

"I know, but …"

She interrupted. "You could always move here if you're so worried."

"I'm not worried. I'm being practical." He studied the lines on both his parents' faces. "What about that speculator nosing around? Out here, you're not as safe."

Mom replied, "We haven't had any more visitors since we told that survey person to leave."

That situation could change. He gripped his fork and kept his mouth shut.

"We've never been scared here before. Why start now?" Pop said. "Those people are worse than roadkill. To hell with them."

Mom added, "We both are good shots, if it comes to that."

"That doesn't make me feel better," Cal said.

She dabbed her lips with a paper napkin. "We appreciate you helping out your dad after his heart trouble. But we don't want to uproot ourselves. Despite what you might think, your father and I are adults who can make measured decisions."

Cal ground his molars together. They'd missed the entire point. "But—"

"I'm getting the custard." Pop pushed back from the table and returned with the serving dish.

Mom absently waved a hand at him, then focused on Cal. "What about your future? What do you want, now that you finished medical school and residency? You're multiple years into practice. Do you want to continue in that direction? What are your goals?"

"It's like I'm talking with a high school guidance counselor."

Pop snorted as he placed the dish in front of Mom. "She needs to aim those skills at someone. Her counseling doesn't work on me."

"You sure about that?" The glare she gave him took his expression from beetle-brow confrontational to innocently contrite in mere seconds.

"Hmm," Pop said.

"So?" Mom asked Cal, spooning up burned custard.

The caramelized sugar called to him as he took the bowl she offered him. "Hadn't given it that much thought." Actually, he had, and that was a big problem.

His brain was crammed full of what-ifs. He'd envisioned every scenario possible, from totally cutting ties with her to going all-in on Team Cal and Deirdre. He wanted to believe that with great risk came great reward, but in this matter, the possibility of failure was way too high.

"Mm-hmm." Like she didn't believe him. "You and Deirdre Steen seem cozy. She could do worse than our son, you know."

Cal laughed. Uncomfortably. "She and I are two old friends hanging out."

In her bed. Naked.

"Your mother and I started off as schoolmate friends, you know."

Cal said, "I know."

Pop waggled an eyebrow and winked. "I was a varsity basketball player in high school. Very popular. Aggie got quite the catch." His eyes glinted. "Out of the bed and in it."

No. Nope. Mom and Pop were *not* reminiscing about

JILLIAN DAVID

sexual history in the same room as Cal. Lines needed to be drawn.

Mom snorted, a faint blush coloring her weathered cheeks. "Anyway, enough about us. You and Deirdre make a wonderful couple. You're both smart, work in healthcare, and what with the tragedy of poor Elijah ..."

"See, that's the problem," Cal blurted out.

"What is?" Mom said.

Pop's eyes narrowed, studying him. Uh-oh.

Sweat prickled his lower back. "Even if I wanted to be more than friends"—and on some level that was his unattainable dream—"I can't compete with a ghost."

"You really think that?"

"I know that."

She rested her chin on her hand. "Elijah was a good person. Everyone liked him."

Cal's stomach sank with every true and damning word.

Mom continued. "You and Elijah are different people, special and good in your own way. You have plenty to bring to the table. Any woman would be lucky to have you in their life."

He squirmed in the wooden chair. "It's easy to say that, but the reality is complicated. Nothing is going to happen with us." Except for last night. Damn. Under the table, he curled his fingers into his thigh.

"I think what your mother is saying is, you have to be open to love. Willing to take a chance. Listen to those around you."

Cal barked a laugh. "Now I know that aliens abducted

the real Pop. I can't believe that the most stubborn person in the state of Alaska gave me that advice. It's rich."

Pop shrugged as he spooned a bite of low-fat custard. "Do as I say not as I do, son."

Chapter Twenty-Two

TUESDAY EVENING'S MEETING with the Koyukon corporation elders, Yukon Valley town leadership, and Ray Mountain landowners left Deirdre fighting not to bite her nails. The nerves had little to do with the topic and her presentation. It had everything to do with the tall frame of the quiet man next to her who radiated both strength and tension.

Calvin and his parents took chairs next to Deirdre and Mav with murmured hellos. She tried to ignore a few craned necks as participants peered at them.

"Hello," Calvin said.

That one whispered word was all it took for Deirdre's toes to tingle. The impact of his low voice right next to her ear the other night, at times murmuring appreciation and then shouting his own release, hit her hard enough to momentarily knock the wind out of her.

He flexed and released his hands on the thighs of his dark brown canvas pants. She couldn't stop staring at those hands. The same hands that had drifted over her, strong but gentle. How those long fingers twined with her own as he drove deep, time and again, until her vision sparkled with her release. She licked her lip but froze at Calvin's sharp turn of his head.

She scanned the room. Tuli Sampson and his grand-mother, Ruth Sampson, sat a few seats down. Ruth, an elder, was looking much better. A few months back, she had been hospitalized with lung problems. Tuli looked better, too, though he walked with a limp and used a cane. She shuddered at the memory of Tuli almost bleeding out in the ED. She glanced at Calvin who had caught Tuli's eye and lifted a brief hand in greeting.

Tuli and his grandmother sat together, murmuring.

EMT Louise Wright entered with her father, elder Steve Wright. He took a seat next to Yukon Valley's mayor. Louise seemed to fade into the group, sitting a row back, though Tuli's head swiveled to follow her movements. Louise settled next to one of the other Ray Mountain landowners who Deirdre vaguely recognized.

Various other elders and town council members sat around the table, along with the local traditional chief. An informational piece of paper lay in front of each person.

After the mayor and the traditional chief gave introductions, the meeting began.

The fifty-year-old elder Steve cleared his throat and adjusted his brown leather vest, the intricate bead patterns of swimming salmon gleaming in the light of the Yukon Valley community center meeting room. "We're here to discuss the concern regarding prospectors trying to gain access to our lands in the greater Yukon Valley area. Maverick and Deirdre Steen, could you share your information, seeing as the speculators targeted your property first?"

"Happy to." Mav sat forward and presented, as he and Deirdre had agreed, given that he had dealt with the outsiders more than she had. "We own several hundred acres west of town, which backs up to a portion of the Ray Mountains. Our property is at the tail end of the range, bordering BLM land. Because of a misfiled Department of Natural Resources survey years ago, our family never knew that there were any provable minerals on our land. Luckily, our original property deed included subsurface mineral rights. Per the information we were given, there may be a vein of gold." He paused and smiled as several faces lit up. "I know. Alaska gold. Everyone wants it. Besides that, and maybe more importantly, the DNR survey assesses that rare earth elements are there."

"What does that mean?" Steve asked.

Several participants took notes.

Deirdre held up a paper as Mav motioned to her. "According to the survey, allanite and monazite, which I had to research. As of a few weeks ago, I had zero idea what these were and why they're important. The names sound strange." Several chuckles popped up. "These are rare earth elements that have a wide range of applications including medical equipment, magnetic properties, and use in nuclear reactors."

Ruth raised her hand. "Do all of the parcels have this ore?"

Deirdre smoothed her button-down navy shirt, aware of all eyes on her, including Calvin's quiet, assessing presence. "Maybe. The DNR survey data in front of you shows the range of likely product is in a roughly east to west vein, north of Yukon Valley proper. The presumed area includes land owned by us, the Garretts, Avilas, Becks, Zieglers, and the corporation."

"Can we make money off of this?" one balding participant asked. Craig Beck. The thirty-something man and his family were third- and fourth-generation Alaskans.

Mav rocked from his heels to the balls of his feet. "We believe that making a profit comes with a price not just in dollars but also in impact to the corporation and our town. It's a big decision that we should carefully weigh, which is why we're all meeting together," he paused. "Extracting the minerals requires access through our lands. Large equipment will be one issue. The other issue is the effect on the landscape. Extraction requires removal of surface land. It won't look the same afterward. Finally, there are environmental concerns."

The traditional chief spoke up from the front. "The corporation and the town have been working on tourism development. Cultural and outdoor tourism. No pun intended, but mismanaging ore extraction could undermine our efforts."

"However, mining could pay for much-needed local infrastructure for tourism and beyond," the mayor said. "More funds for schools, museums, lodging, restaurants."

Many heads nodded.

"There will be a lot of hands out, hoping for a piece of the pie," Steve said. "From my earlier days, I know about the impact of gold mining with mercury and arsenic in high amounts in the water supply. As stewards of our land, I don't want to do anything to risk the unique beauty of this area or the safety of everyone living here. What about those other minerals? Are they safe to mine?"

Deirdre continued, "Allanite, depending on the form, has radioactive properties. This is not uncommon in rare earth elements. From what I was able to find out, excavating radioactive material could contaminate the land and waterways." She rustled the paper. "Granted, I am not an expert in radioactive minerals or rare earth elements."

A heavy silence fell on the room. This group of people lived off the land and respected the waterways, whether for cultural, recreational, or commercial reasons. No one here wanted to risk ruining their home. Yet, the promise of money was a strong motivator, and it could improve people's lives in other ways.

"So, the question is twofold," the mayor said, folding her hands in front of her. "First, do we want the prospectors to come here, and if so, how many and for what price? Or could we prospect on our own and benefit more directly? Second, if we do grant them access to our land, how can we guarantee the safety of our water, preserve the tourism economy, and still get something in return to help our town?"

Chatter rose and fell around her. Calvin remained silent.

"What if we leave it be?" Bruce spoke up. "A DNR assessor was sniffing around our place recently. I mean, look what that other guy tried to pull on Maverick to get his land."

Mav added, "My guess is that the speculators will keep trying to gain access to one or more parcels of someone's land that abuts the Ray Mountains."

"It'd be nice if they gave up," Bruce grumbled.

Calvin's voice cut through the room as he leaned forward. "They might give up. For a time. When they return in a year or two or more, then what?"

Ruth sat forward. "What if our land's value can benefit our town and our children and grandchildren?" She patted Tuli on the leg and he sheepishly smiled.

"That's a valid possibility," Steve said.

Deirdre held very still, Mav and Calvin doing the same on either side of her. It wasn't one person's decision. The implications of having a large mining company here could have ramifications, both positive and negative.

Steve turned to Mav and Deirdre. "You've dealt with these people. What did you think?"

"Honestly, my opinion is not fit to be printed," Mav said as everyone laughed. "Randy Nelson tried to bankrupt us and steal our property. About as dishonorable as a person can be."

Deirdre added, "They were real jerks. I wouldn't trust them farther than I could throw them."

Calvin looked at her for a beat, then raised his hand. "I recently spoke with the lead guy, Randy, to get more information. Let's say, he wasn't pleasant to deal with."

Funny, his words versus her recollection of Calvin and Randy shaking hands... those two things didn't jive. Deirdre held still, straining to hear everything he said, every nuance, every intonation. Her neck itched. Something didn't quite add up.

Calvin leaned forward. "Is there a guaranteed way we can protect the land for future generations? Or is it best to go ahead and grant access but control the impact? They are going to eventually get in there one way or another."

Lots of murmured yesses.

The mayor held up a hand. "That's one option for how we approach this situation."

Steve frowned and tapped his pen on the table. "Whatever we do, it should be together. That's hard, because in a room of people, that's how many opinions there are. Any wavering in our plan, those people will come in and exploit our weakness, regardless of what most of us want."

Deirdre said, "Mav and I have decided we won't let go of our land or grant access, especially to Randy and his team. Any chance other property owners will stand with us?"

Craig Beck piped up, "I wouldn't mind getting money for my kids' college fund, but I'll hold off for now until I see how we can all benefit from these minerals."

Then the Avilas, the elders, the Zieglers, and the Garretts all agreed to pause any decisions to allow access for now.

Ruth said, "Motion to create a working group of involved and interested parties to study this question further. Recommend that we agree to proceed as one voice in the future."

The future. Deirdre glanced at Calvin while those in the meeting discussed the subcommittee. She hadn't given much thought to what her own future might look like. Not since Elijah died. Burying herself in work, and now helping Mav with the lodge, kept her too busy to do much more than tread water.

Calvin glanced over at her with a smile that looked both heated and regretful. Then he looked away.

How easy had it been to envision a future, working together with him and helping to care for the place she loved—both with respect to the mining potential on her property and with local healthcare.

That personal future—the one with Calvin as a partner building a life with her—she couldn't even consider that possibility.

Actually, she *had* considered that possibility more than once. It scared the hell out of her.

It wasn't the possibility that scared her. It was the chance of losing her future again. Deep in thought, she zoned out through the remainder of the discussion.

After the meeting ended, Calvin turned toward her and murmured, "Good to see you."

A shiver slid up her back. "You, too."

"Still up for dinner tomorrow night?"

"Is it fake or real?" she said, low enough that only he could hear.

"Depends on what you want."

Her face heated as the people around them—Bruce, Aggie, and Mav—sat way too quiet and still. "Send me the details."

Maybe this was the right person. Maybe she could trust herself to take a risk and see if a future could happen for her and Calvin, after all.

"Will do." He briefly touched her arm, then dropped his hand and turned toward his parents and the other people present.

Chapter Twenty-Three

T HE NEXT DAY Cal stopped to catch his breath after chopping another cord of wood at his parents' place. He checked his watch. 5:25 p.m. He'd need to jump in the shower soon if he was going to be on time to pick up Deirdre for dinner at 6. Nothing like keeping up appearances to fake date the woman he had not-fake slept with.

No. They were truly dating. Problem was, neither of them would acknowledge that it was real.

He rubbed his sweaty brow and took off his fleece jacket, hanging it off a hook sticking out from the side of the metal garage. Rolling up his flannel sleeves, he exhaled and let the clean, crisp air flow over him.

He hated pushing Deirdre, but for his own mental state they needed to talk through this situation and decide together how to proceed. Tonight, then.

Pulling out his phone he texted, "*Still on for dinner?*" Thank God the homestead had been finally set up with satellite internet Wi-Fi so he could make calls and text.

A few seconds later, she replied, "*Yes ... finishing work at Mom and Pop's. No change in your plans?*"

He chuckled. "*At this point it would be an act of God for me to no show.*"

Her response. *"Not reassuring!"*

He laughed out loud and stowed the phone in his pants pocket.

Deirdre always made him smile. On the one hand, he could picture himself seeing her lovely face every day. On the other hand, his lingering self-doubt about measuring up to Elijah and the potential impact to his career in Seattle stopped him cold.

He hated to admit it, but at the end of the day, it might be that he and Deirdre were different people in different places in their lives with different priorities. Right people, wrong time. Damn, if that ended up being the case, it would suck.

Could he accept that reality? He had a lot to think about.

Thankfully, with his folks and Doofus gone to Fairbanks, Cal had used the day to clear his mind with some physical work.

His folks weren't going to move, and that was that. No amount of Cal's nudges would change that fact. He had failed in his mission, but at the end of the day, they had to live their own lives on their own terms.

Cal now understood all too well what that meant.

In the meeting yesterday, it had struck him how much everyone cared about not only the land but the community as a whole and each other. The fierce independence of the Alaskans in that room, combined with their determination to help out their neighbors for the good of this area, gave him even more to consider.

A week ago, Cal had done what he thought was right to

keep his parents and Deirdre safe, but now? He looked over the high mountains on one horizon and low hills sweeping down to the icy Yukon River on the other side. He sniffed and rolled up a sleeve that had loosened. Somehow, he would fix what he'd done.

Cal picked up the axe and continued making wood. He might not be able to move his parents to a safer location, but he could at least provide fuel for heat. The bar for accomplishments as a son had been set pretty low lately.

After another few minutes of chopping, he stretched tired muscles in his back and inhaled fresh, cool air. Temps had hit fifty earlier today. The beginning of April wasn't a guarantee of no snow in Alaska's interior, but the longer, warmer days teased the brief summer to come. Lots of snow melting today. He shifted his boots on the graveled area where he made his woodpile. There was less mud here than everywhere else on the property, but it still clogged the lugs of his boots.

A vehicle rumbled up the dirt road. Calvin planted his axe in the chopping block and walked around to the front of the house. As he came around the corner, a tan SUV with lots of mud spatter on the wheel wells idled in the driveway.

A familiar forty-something man got out and smiled too-broadly. "Howdy."

"Randy. What are you doing here?" He kept his tone civil, but cool.

"Your folks home?"

A second man, taller and younger appearing by his movements and clad in a drab-colored jacket, exited the

SUV. Cal squinted. Looked like a DNR logo. Then a tall woman who looked to be in her early thirties, also wearing a puffy coat, too warm for today's temps, stepped out of the vehicle.

A warm rush of adrenaline shot through Cal as his heartrate picked up. He surreptitiously patted his cargo pants pocket to ensure the gun he kept on him for bears was still in place.

"They're out. What can I do for you?" He kept his voice low and firm.

This guy and his friends needed to get off of his parents' property. Now.

He lifted his hands. "Hey, I'm just paying a friendly visit to finalize my generous offer."

Like hell. "You and I have already talked."

"I hadn't heard from you. It's time to review my options for access. If you aren't agreeable, then someone else will be." He strolled toward the front porch.

Calvin angled his stride to intercept Randy. No way would he let the guy in the house. He wanted this guy and his friends to leave. Would have been nice if he had the axe in his hand right now. Or bear spray. He preferred not to actually shoot anyone.

"Pretty sure my parents or I don't have business with you," he said.

Randy unzipped his jacket and pulled out a folder. "Pretty sure we do have business. Here's the final paperwork, like you and I discussed. These are my witnesses."

The other man and the woman strolled too casually past

Randy over to the side of the house. They murmured quietly. The woman curled her lip as her suede boots squelched on the wet gravel.

The hairs on the back of Cal's neck stood up. He could use Doofus right now. At least the mutt could distract Randy by slobbering on the guy. Cal pivoted so he could keep everyone in his field of vision. "Changed my mind. There's nothing for us to discuss. I've got your number. I'll tell my parents you called."

Randy frowned and took a step toward Cal. "When are they getting back?"

"Hard to say." No way was he giving that information.

He'd stay here and guard the place until they returned from Fairbanks. Longer, if need be.

Randy held the file out, then paused and backed up next to the SUV. "Here's the information."

Cal kept the man and woman in his peripheral vision as he walked toward Randy.

Randy continued. "See, I need you to finish this paper-work. Before anyone else gets hurt. Like the Steens."

Deirdre? Maverick? Sweat chilled on his neck. "I don't follow." He laid the paper on the hood and flipped through the pages to the signature page which Randy had already signed.

"You and I had a deal," Randy said. "The sooner we get access to the range, the sooner we'll be out of everyone's hair."

"We never made a deal."

"Seemed like it from where I sat." He spat and crossed

his arms. "Look, if I'm not allowed access despite my reasonable request, then maybe it's time to send a message."

The woman moved to Randy's left and slowly put her hand in her coat.

Cal's heart thudded fast enough to feel winded. *Run*, his brain urged him. If they had guns, he was outmanned.

Best to keep the conversation going so he could think a way out of this situation. "What does that have to do with people getting hurt? I don't follow." He tensed, ready to bolt or fight, while he kept his eyes on the woman's movements.

Randy put his hands in his pockets. "You will."

A light footfall crunched behind him. As Cal turned toward the sound, a blinding pain exploded in his head, and everything went soundless and black.

Chapter Twenty-Four

DEIRDRE TAPPED HER fingers on the wood veneer of the diner table and sighed. Six thirty and no sign of Calvin.

At first, her nervousness had come from preparing to talk with Calvin about the decision she had made about their relationship. It was time to reach for happiness. Time to push back against doubt. Time to face her fears and see if Calvin was on the same page.

If they weren't on the same page?

At least she could feel proud to have put her heart on the line and taken a risk, which was more than she had been able to do the past four years.

However, to have the conversation required both parties' attendance. She sipped water and tried not to meet the waitress's sympathetic gaze. She ignored the murmurs of other customers. Deirdre checked her phone once more.

No answer to her latest text from five minutes ago. Or ten minutes ago.

Irritation and embarrassment prickled her skin. Her face heated up. Damn it, she had made an effort to look nice this evening. Even pulled out a wine-colored silk blouse and gray slacks combo she rarely wore. She checked the phone again.

Nothing.

Was this a subtle hint? She could handle that.

Only, Calvin had always replied, even when he was frustrated with her. This was damned unusual.

Now she knew his usual patterns? He probably had a good reason to be gone. An emergency must have come up at the hospital.

Deirdre called and spoke with Amberlyn who was the nurse on shift right now in the ED. No sign of Calvin. No patients in the department.

Another quick call to Mav. No EMS calls in the past hour.

She bit her lip and glanced at the door for the thousandth time. Where was he? Maybe she was a worrywart, but something was wrong.

Standing, she tugged on her light jacket. The sun was still above the horizon. It was cool outside, but not frigid cold. After leaving a few dollars for the water and the waitress's time, she left.

Ten minutes later, Deirdre pulled up in front of Bruce and Aggie's place, heart rattling in time with the Subaru's wheels on the dirt road. No lights shone in the windows of the house.

She stepped out.

Silence, except for a slight breeze through the spruce trees. No barking dog. Calvin's car was parked off to the side, but there no sign of the Garretts's vehicle.

She looked around. Where was Calvin?

Her heart hammered in her chest. Hundreds of scenarios

flew by her: an accident, a bear, a heart attack.

"Calvin?" she called as she crept toward the house.

Nothing.

She tried the front door. Unlocked. Knocking loudly as she entered, she called out again and quickly checked all of the rooms. Empty. Everything seemed in order.

In the shadow cast by the angle of the setting sun, she peeked through a window and spied a figure on the side of the house across from the woodpile, sprawled on the ground. Her heart thumped hard, stealing her breath.

No!

Deirdre dashed out and around the house, skidding to a stop. Calvin lay prone, arms extended above him and legs straight. There were drag marks from his feet around to the front of the house. He wasn't moving. Was he breathing? She checked his pulse above the neckline of his dark flannel shirt and noted his torso rise.

Her breath rasped in her throat. She couldn't draw in enough air. "Calvin?" She patted his back and shoulder. "Calvin?"

Not even a moan returned. The back of his head was matted with sticky blood. She grunted as she rolled him in one movement, keeping his head and neck in line, unhappy that he had to lay in slush and mud. The side of his face that had been pressed against the wet gravel was clammy and red. His lips were blue.

But he breathed.

His shirt was wet and muddy on the front. She grimaced at the damp ground beneath him. Now the shirt was wet and muddy on the back as well. His hair-dusted forearms and strong hands rested on the ground, completely lax. He didn't move.

Yanking out her phone, she prayed that her phone still remembered the Garretts's Wi-Fi password so she could call out with the satellite internet. She dialed 911 and nearly cried in relief when the trooper picked up. Quickly, she gave the information to dispatch.

She carefully opened Calvin's eyelids. No pupillary response. Icy terror rushed through her from head to toe. Her ears buzzed.

Oh God, not again. She couldn't lose someone she cared for. Not like this. Not Calvin.

Stay, she mentally begged him. Like Elijah had asked her, five years ago.

Stay.

She needed Calvin to survive this.

She could help him right now. Deirdre needed to work the problem. Assess the situation.

He was breathing. He had a pulse.

He was also cold and wet. His last text was over an hour ago, so she could calculate the maximum length of time he had laid here. Too long. He was too cold. Hypothermic.

She peeled off her jacket and tucked it over him. Then she spied his jacket near the woodpile and dashed over to grab it and place it around his hips and thighs, providing reasonable cover from neck to knees.

"Calvin?" she tried again.

He made an incoherent mumble, then went silent, puffing air between his blue lips with quick, shallow breaths.

Hurry, EMS. Hurry. Tears flowed as she shook in her boots.

The memory of Elijah's withered and comatose body, failing in its last hours, superimposed itself on Calvin's injured form. She couldn't watch this. Couldn't be here. This was too much. Her chest ached. It hurt to breathe. She curled her fingers around her car keys and glanced toward the front of the house where she had parked. The need to escape this pain overwhelmed her.

No.

She would stay.

Her face went numb. Blood-chilling panic drove her.

Dashing into the house, she yanked a throw blanket and cushion off the couch and ran back out, tucking the blanket over and around him and easing the cushion under his head. That was about all she could do at this point. Basic care and support until he could get proper evaluation.

She rechecked his weak, fast pulse and increased breathing rate.

Hurry.

What felt like hours later, a vehicle pulled up. She ran to the front of the house and directed the EMS crew. An Alaska state trooper vehicle pulled up next to the ambulance.

Mav and Louise jumped out, bags in hand.

Mav frowned at Deirdre. "What happened?"

They hurried to Calvin. "No idea. Found him down. I don't know how long he's been out. Guessing he's hypothermic." Last text was 5:25. She checked her phone. It was now a few minutes before seven.

Ninety minutes he could have been laying here.

Mav removed the blanket and jackets to do a quick primary assessment, then he and Louise applied EKG leads and obtained vitals. Sats were low, but then again Calvin's fingers were freezing, so there wasn't enough tissue perfusion to get a good signal. Deirdre chafed his cold hands between hers, willing him to warm up.

To wake up.

After putting on a cervical collar and applying oxygen, Mav and Louise got him onto the backboard and loaded onto the gurney. Calvin groaned slightly.

"Well, that adds a point on the GCS," Mav quipped with a grim press of his mouth.

Glasgow Coma Scale. Damn it. Deirdre's past and present collided, and her knees nearly buckled if not for Lieutenant Kate Lucas's grip on her upper arm.

"Let's go," Louise said, pulling the gurney across the uneven ground, Mav pushing.

"Are you going to the hospital, too?" Mav asked.

Deirdre shrugged. "Technically, I'm not family, but his parents aren't here. What do you think?"

"We're all family here. Besides, a friendly face wouldn't be the worst thing for him to see when he wakes up. You can update Bruce and Aggie, as well."

"Fair enough." She didn't want to pull too much rank, but she did want to be there for him. They were dating. Kind of. Fake dating. Sort of real. Who cared? She would be with him. With that decision, she would risk their relationship being real. Damn it.

Before following the ambulance to the hospital, Deirdre called Aggie and explained the situation. Aggie and Bruce would stay in Fairbanks overnight. If they left now, they'd be driving back four hours in the dark. For safety, Deirdre encouraged them to stay there tonight and return early tomorrow. Deirdre promised to remain with Calvin and provide updates.

"We know you care about him, and he cares about you,' Aggie said.

She hated the pretense. The wasted time. Hated how her heart ached at Calvin's too-still form. The last peg fell into place in her heart. She did care for him. She could admit it and not feel guilt or pain.

The freedom that realization brought gave her a little light within this dark situation. "You're right."

Before leaving, Deirdre gave her account to the state trooper. Well, what little she knew about the situation. Nothing seemed amiss with the house other than Calvin lying injured and unconscious next to the building. It didn't appear anything had been broken into by man or animal. Vehicle and footprints weren't easily visible due to the slushy, wet gravel. What had happened?

With a tight, professional nod, Lieutenant Kate stowed her pad and pencil in a pocket. "I'll find out if anything else seems out of place in town. Then I'll check back with him in the hospital. Hopefully he'll be awake and can give a statement."

A quick hug, and Kate followed her from the Garrett

homestead down to town.

Gripping the wheel with shaking hands, Deirdre somehow managed to safely steer her car down the road toward the highway. Turning up the heat in her car, she shivered without her jacket while the air slowly increased in temperature. The heat didn't take away the bone-deep chills racing through her.

Once at the hospital, Mav and Louise, the nurses, and Dr. Tipton all efficiently tended to Calvin in the trauma bay. Deirdre fought against the gut need to be at the bedside helping. Instead, she planted her butt in a work area chair and tried not to overhear what was being said.

A few minutes later, Mav came over to give her a quick hug before saying, "Sorry I can't stick around, sis. We've got another call." He and Louise rushed out of the ED.

Murmurs and beeps filtered back to her from Calvin's room.

A few minutes later as he was wheeled out for a CT scan, he turned his head and squinted at her. "Deirdre." He slurred the word, eyes half open.

She shot up from her seat and stood next to him. "Hey, you're awake. I'm right here." Taking care with the IVs in place, she grasped his hand. "Your folks know what's going on."

"Dinner?"

She glanced at Amberlyn and Clyde, who both immediately studied some patterns on the floor.

"Typical, huh?" she said. "I keep saying how our crazy schedules don't line up well these days."

JILLIAN DAVID

"Deirdre." A faint smile shifted his expression. "Stay." His voice was a few decibels above a whisper.

Tears burned behind her eyelids, but somehow Deirdre held herself together. "Oh, sure," she said too lightly. "I'll be right here when you get back from CT."

"Talk later. Scan now," Dr. Tipton scolded gently.

Her concerned, tight expression belied the soft tone of voice. She was worried.

Calvin winced. "I make a terrible patient."

"You're not wrong." The doctor tapped her foot. "Let's get this taken care of. Then if you're nice, I'll let you read your own radiology images." After the nurses wheeled him away to the scanner, she turned to Deirdre and studied her for several seconds. With a sigh, she said, "Technically, I can't tell you anything as you're not family."

"I won't ask. Don't worry."

"He talked to you, which is good. Also, he said he wants you in the room. So later, when you're in the room with him per his request, if you happened to overhear me discussing his condition and my findings, then so be it."

"Thanks, Dr. Tipton."

She gave Deirdre a quick hug. "You can call me Lee, you know."

"Yes, but not in a professional setting."

She patted Deirdre on the upper arm. "You know, you don't always have to be on the clock or setting a good example. Sometimes it's okay for people to know you're human."

Deirdre rocked back on her heels. All of the work she did

210

day in and day out to make this hospital chug along, to train and employ excellent nurses and other staff, to maintain safety and professionalism—it really had dug into her entire psyche.

Dedication to the job had become another form of armor. Protective, yes, but it also insulated Deirdre from everyone around her. Professionalism had kept her from dealing with the more painful parts of her life. There wasn't much else to say but, "Point taken. Thank you." Deirdre wandered to the back of the ED work area. She sat down hard and thought even harder about so many parts of her life.

Twenty minutes later, the automatic doors to radiology opened, and staff wheeled Calvin back to his room. He beckoned for Deirdre to join them, and she eased in after them and pulled up a chair at the bedside. He reached out and she laced her fingers with his.

After the leads had been reattached and another set of vitals reassured everyone, Deirdre asked him, "What happened?"

It seemed like his eyes took a few seconds to focus on her. He squinted, like the dim light was still too bright. "I don't completely remember," he mumbled, speech and mouth movements sluggish. "Last thing I remember was Randy pulling up. He wanted to talk about access to the property." His eyes popped open. "Two other people got out of that car. Then *blammo*, lights out. This"—he waved his hand weakly—"could have happened to one of my parents."

Deirdre's blood iced. Randy did this? He was more determined than she had expected. Now, he brought friends and had hurt Calvin. Who else would he harm to get what he wanted?

She sent Mav a text to keep his eyes open and check the lodge and the dog team. Then she sent a vague and HIPAA-compliant text to Steve Wright so he could have the people in the Koyukon village stay extra vigilant. He promised to give the other property owners and the mayor a heads-up as well.

"I know this is not how you planned to spend the evening," Calvin said.

Despite the situation, her face warmed. "There are worse ways to spend it."

"Thank you for being here."

"Your parents will arrive tomorrow midday. They're worried about you. Hope you don't mind but I've been sending them updates."

"Of course." He turned his head and groaned.

"You okay?"

"Dizzy every time I move my head. It takes a few seconds for my brain to process what I'm seeing or hearing. It's like walking through mud, mentally." His half-pained chuckle made her heart flop. "Now I have more sympathy for patients with head injuries."

"Not that you needed any. You're pretty compassionate."

"Says who?"

"Says your initial Press-Ganey patient satisfaction scores."

His face, still half ruddy from the cold exposure, creased

in an uneven smile. "Are you ever not on the clock as an administrator?"

"*Hmph.*" She let go of his hand and held up a finger. "Hang on while I answer this text from your mother." She paused, typed, and said out loud, "They're all settled in for the evening at the hotel in Fairbanks."

"Good." He blinked and winced. "Say, can you dim the lights some more? It's really bright."

She frowned at the low lights but lowered them even further. "Sure."

Dr. Tipton stepped into the room. "Knock, knock. How are you feeling?" Her thoughtful expression encompassed both Deirdre and Calvin and the dim light.

"Frankly? Confused and fuzzy. Head hurts like a beast. Chunks of my memory seem to be missing." Once again, he reached for Deirdre's hand. "What's the prognosis?"

"So, radiologist says this is a subdural hematoma."

"Well, that's better than epidural hematoma."

"True. You want to see the scan?" Dr. Tipton turned toward the computer screen.

"No. The light bothers me, and I don't think that I can focus. Or that I should try to," he said.

"That's reasonable." She paused, concern drawing her light brows together. "So. You probably know the drill. I spoke with the neurologist in Fairbanks."

"Is it big enough that they need to do a burr hole?" he said. "Like I need a hole in my head, huh?" How could he joke at a time like this?

Deirdre squeezed his hand.

Dr. Tipton gave a brief chuckle. "If you needed to have pressure relieved emergently, the chopper would already be en route to fly you out." She wiggled her fingers at him. "And before you ask, no, I won't do it myself. Unlike you fancy ED doctor-types, this family doc doesn't want to do major surgery at the bedside."

"Admit it. For a second, you thought about it."

The secret smile she gave sent a shiver down Deirdre's spine.

"Fairbanks was prepared to walk me through it." Oh God, she was serious.

Deirdre spoke up. "Okay, you cowboys. No more discussion of brain surgery in Yukon Valley. Please. You two are a little scary in how much you seem to like this stuff."

"Inappropriate humor makes hard things better," he said.

"The fact that you can make jokes is reassuring," Dr. Tipton said. "We need to watch you overnight. Neuro checks every hour."

He nodded and glanced at Deirdre, explaining. "This could be my lucid interval. With epidurals the window of clarity is generally four hours. With subdural hematomas, there's no upper limit to the time when the subdural could suddenly expand." He explained it like he was teaching a medical student. Clinical. Objective.

Deirdre processed the information. She couldn't breathe.

He was saying that he could quickly get worse and lose brain function or die. That was no joke. "Shouldn't you be in Fairbanks, then? Closer to the specialist?"

"Neuro didn't think so, though I'm happy to push for

transfer if you want," Dr. Tipton said. "They felt that the subdural was small. The chance of progression is low, and weather looks good if you have to fly in the next few days. We have good options available right now. In the meantime, we'll rescan in twelve hours. If the neuro exam changes or the subdural grows, then you'll get that complimentary trip to Fairbanks."

Calvin nodded, with a wince. "Good."

Deirdre unwrapped her fingers tightly clutched around his.

Dr. Tipton continued, "As for the hypothermia, you seem to be doing much better with the warmed fluids and the heated-air blanket. We'll continue with telemetry monitoring overnight, but the chance of an arrythmia is low at this point."

Calvin smiled. "Much appreciation for your choice of monitoring my temperature, by the way."

The doctor actually giggled. "True. If you hadn't regained consciousness or telemetry showed abnormal rhythms, you know which core temperature probe I'd be using."

"Yowch." Calvin's eyebrows shot up, then he gave an exaggerated wince.

Dr. Tipton glanced back behind her at low voices coming from the work area. "Law enforcement wants to talk with you at some point. I'll need to provide them my medical findings."

"Share any information they need. I can give my statement now." His gray eyes met Deirdre's for a second. "That way, if my condition changes, they have the necessary information."

Despite the warmth in the room, a chill walked bony fingers down Deirdre's spine.

If his condition changes.

If his subdural expands and he dies.

Calvin wasn't in the clear yet.

"Right. Let's get you tucked in for the evening. As luck would have it, I'm also your attending doctor for admission." She did a jazz hands move. "Ta-da, rural medicine." Then she turned and exited.

He locked eyes with Deirdre again. "I am a lucky guy in more ways than one."

Air lodged in her lungs and wouldn't budge. Deirdre had witnessed luck fail in the face of relentlessly progressing medical conditions.

She knew, better than most, that luck might not be enough.

But by God, she was going to remain by his side.

Chapter Twenty-Five

ONCE IN THE med-surg inpatient room, Cal wrapped up the questions with Lieutenant Kate and let his body relax into the bed, trying his best to appreciate the one-size-fit-nobody hospital gown with complimentary air conditioning in the back. Before doing the first of the evening's many neuro checks, the nurse had turned on the air cushion feature. Good news was he wouldn't get a pressure ulcer. Bad news? It felt like he was sleeping on a shifting marshmallow.

Things could be worse.

He squinted in the low light and spied Deirdre, who half sat, half reclined on the vinyl loveseat, her head drooping. Her chin-length brown hair, normally styled, was a tangled mess, like she'd run her hands through it more than once. Despite the low light in the patient room, that silky maroon shirt of hers made her skin glow.

She was beautiful.

She was here. With him.

Calvin's chest squeezed.

It took a brain injury, a brief coma, and getting admitted to his own hospital to wake Calvin up to a few key truths.

One, the comfort and *rightness* that Deirdre's presence brought him was more than friendship. More than fake dating. Their connection was real. His desire to have her in his life was real.

Two, they were not the same people as when they were eighteen years old. Different priorities. Different history.

Three, he realized that he wasn't second best to his best friend. It wasn't a competition. He was the right guy at this time. If that meant the possibility of a future with Deirdre, he could accept that reality.

He turned his head, gritting his teeth against the head-spinning nausea and the ever-present headache.

She sighed, then lifted her head. "How are you doing?" Her tired smile triggered a deep-seated need to wrap her in his arms so that she could rest.

"You can go home if you need to," he said.

She scrubbed her eyes. "No, I can stay. If you're okay with that."

"Very okay. There's no one I'd rather have here."

Hard to tell if she blushed in the dim light.

She shoved hair behind her ear. "Um, I'll text your mom with another update."

"Hopefully, that keeps them from worrying."

She typed and nodded. "All done."

"Deirdre."

She froze, phone in hand, eyes wide. "Are you okay?"

"Stop worrying. I'm stable." He studied her. "Who worries about you, Deirdre?"

"Sorry, what?"

"My parents fret about me."

"Their job is to worry. They're your parents."

"True. I'm sure Mav checks in with you."

"Of course. When he's not living his own life." She frowned and he wanted to smooth those lines with a fingertip. "Where are you going with this?"

"You're so busy looking after everyone else." He locked her gaze with his. "Who cares for you when you need it? When you're hurt."

The catch in her breath and stricken expression came and went in a split second. "I don't have a head injury or living parents, so I'm fine." Her voice cracked. "Thanks for asking."

She huffed and rearranged the water container and the TV remote on the bedside stand. The busyness didn't mask the shimmer in her eyes.

Fine, she could avoid the subject for now. But not forever.

Her prickly response to his probing questions actually made him feel more normal. It made the relationship seem real.

It *was* real. He hadn't fully realized it until right now.

"So sorry we missed dinner tonight," he said.

"You had a good excuse." She pulled a chair up next to the bed, so they were at eye level. "It's okay, Calvin. We don't have to pretend to date."

"No more pretending."

A flicker of pain creased her forehead. "We shouldn't be having this conversation here. You are concussed. You need to rest."

Something shifted inside of him. "My skull might be

cracked, but I know what I want." He reached for her hand. "I'm tired of wasting time and avoiding the truth."

He deserved happiness, and this was his chance.

Damn. Hitting his head had apparently knocked some sense loose. Or activated the part of his brain that forced him to get in touch with his feelings and face his fears. He swallowed.

Deirdre's gaze slid to their joined hands. "Well, let's start by talking about our game plan for the Breakup Festival."

After a few seconds, he squeezed her hand as his eyelids dropped. "Okay. We'll begin there," he mumbled. "Eventually, we still need to discuss *us*."

"Deal."

Chapter Twenty-Six

A FEW DAYS later on Sunday morning, Deirdre's phone rang, shooting her from half asleep to sitting bolt upright in mere seconds. A wave of sweat dampened her flannel pajamas; her heart pounded. Glancing at the clock, she grimaced. 9:32 a.m. She looked around. She was in her own house. Not in the hospital.

For the first time in a long time, she had slept in. It was a miracle. No personal emergencies, no last-minute staffing issues, no need to cover at the lodge.

Following on the heels of relief was an icy spike of fear as the phone rang again. Calvin. Her heart stuttered. No, it was okay. This was Calvin. He was alive. His CT scans and neuro evaluations had been stable.

After his parents had arrived in the hospital Thursday morning, she had gone to work, like any other day. He had been discharged that afternoon.

Then Friday morning before work, she had stopped by Bruce and Aggie's to briefly visit with Calvin. See? He was fine then, too.

But … there was always the chance that something could change.

God, at what point would she stop letting fear control

her?

Pulling in a deep breath, she answered the call. "Calvin? Are you okay?"

"Good morning," he said.

Her body went limp. All she could think to say was, "Glad you didn't text."

"Well, hello to you as well. I could text if I wanted to." His voice reached out to her like an embrace she craved.

Involuntarily, she inclined her body toward the phone. "You're on brain rest for the next week. No screen time. Doctor's orders."

"It's boring. Also, Mom and Pop are kind of driving me crazy. I can only take so many naps. Or listen to Pop explain why everything is wrong with the entire world and how it could be fixed if only someone would listen to his ideas." His parents had insisted that he stay with them for a week. The plan was for him to return to the hospital's rental house this Thursday. "They won't even let me watch TV. It's torture."

With a flash, she leaned toward the phone, wanting to be the one to help with his recovery. Deirdre froze. That impulse was a revelation she needed to examine. Later.

She tucked her hair behind her ear. "Oh, let them dote. It gives them a project to work on, and you need to rest and recover."

"I know."

Her heart squeezed at his weary, defeated tone. This vital, active, smart guy had to feel stifled in every area of his existence right now.

He didn't need her to amplify his frustration, so she

focused on the positive. "Hey, the elders were updated about Randy and his friends' troublemaking. Lieutenant Kate and her state troopers from the Yukon Valley office are looking for the guy, but he's nowhere to be found."

"Has anyone else been threatened or hurt?" Classic Calvin, looking out for people's safety.

"Thankfully, no. Maybe he decided to drop his plans for good."

"We should be so lucky," he said heatedly.

"Oh yes." She lay back down in the still-warm bed and pulled up the blankets to ward off the chill. What she'd give to have Calvin's arms around her, warming her instead. She sighed. "In good news, it appears all the stakeholders from our meeting are in agreement to deny Randy or any other prospectors access to the land. The community is going to do this as a team. They want to understand more about the pros and cons of the resources and vet possible companies that can safely extract the minerals. The working group will drive the decision-making."

"Good. I wouldn't gift Randy the mud off the bottom of my shoes."

"He's bad news."

"No kidding. Hopefully, he'll stay out of town for good." His soul-deep exhale coming right through her phone triggered goose bumps on her arms.

"Maybe he'll take the hint when law enforcement catches up with him."

"That guy will only take a hint if he's in prison." The phone jostled, like he was walking somewhere. A door closed. "Are you being safe?"

"Yes."

"Can you check?" he said, voice low.

The level of caution was understandable. "I'll check again." She got out of bed, shivered in her PJ's, and hurried to her front door and back door to make sure they were locked. "Everything is secure." Settling on the couch, she pulled up a throw blanket.

"Good. I don't like you being alone with Randy still out there. By now, he's probably made the connection between the lodge property, Maverick, me and my parents, and you."

With good friends and neighbors around, Deirdre had always felt safe living on her own in Yukon Valley. Until recently. She glanced toward the living room window. Yes, she would prefer to have Calvin here with her, but it was too soon for that. Besides, head injury.

"Deirdre, are you still there?"

"Yes." She rubbed her hand over her face and pulled the blanket up under her chin, keeping the phone next to her ear.

Silence drifted between them.

"So, how are you doing?" he asked in that warm tone of voice that wrapped around her like a thick duvet.

"That's my question for you."

He paused, as if he wanted to challenge her deflection, then answered. "Better. Lee has me out of work for another two weeks, but I can start back to non-exertional activities now. Then driving and light exertion in a few days. Woo-hoo." He finished with a deprecating laugh. "It's hard following instructions. I make a crappy patient. Do as I say, not as I do."

"You're not wrong."

"Thanks."

"So? Light exertion sounds like a win."

His voice dropped down an octave. "I wouldn't mind doing some light exertion with you."

"Why are you whispering?"

"Because I'm a grown adult in his childhood bedroom, phone flirting with another grown adult. I'd put money on one or both parents listening from the other side of the door. This right here is why adult children and parents should not live with each other."

Laughing, she said, "Ooh, I can imagine Bruce and Aggie with their ears pressed to the door."

"Wouldn't put it past them." He cleared his throat. "But I don't want to talk about my parents." His words bordered on a sexy growl, and she liked it.

"Okay." Her heart thudded. She rubbed her legs together. The pajamas had become way too warm. She threw back the blanket to cool off.

"So. Light exertion?"

Were they really having this conversation? Deirdre couldn't remember the last time she had been truly flirtatious. It was fun. "Oh, but what about your brain?"

"Screw my brain. Literally."

A big laugh erupted from her, and she slapped a hand over her mouth. "That's hilarious!"

"You didn't answer my question." There was a rustle of

sheets as he shifted. "When I'm medically released, would you be okay if I drove to your house and thanked you for saving my life?"

"Hmm," she hedged, enjoying the teasing.

"I'd really like to show my appreciation. I'm *very* appreciative."

"Wow." Her neck heated up. "Yes."

He pressed. "What's on your mind, Deirdre?"

"You called me." For some reason, she couldn't stop smiling.

Of course, he couldn't see her expression.

"If you haven't figured it out, I miss you."

Running a finger over her lips, she said, "Can you be more specific?"

"Tough audience." He breathed and it felt like he was right next to her. "I miss your smile. Your strength. Your brains. Your ... body."

"Well. It's hard to argue with all of that."

His chuckle echoed her tingling desire. "Speaking of hard." He groaned. "Apparently, the head injury didn't cause other organ damage."

Unable to suppress a snort, she added, "It's possible that the head injury has disinhibited you!"

"This is me, enjoying talking with you. Has nothing to do with any frontal lobe damage." He laughed, then lowered his voice again. "I'd like to do more than talk."

"Well, if we think that's safe ..."

"We'll have to find out, won't we?"

"Oh my."

After a few seconds of chuckling together, he said, "Let's talk about the festival coming up. With everyone around."

Instinctively, she stiffened. "Okay."

"I'm not sure if I want to go on with the way things are between us."

"Sure. With your head injury, that's understandable."

"No. As a fake dating couple."

"Oh." She rubbed her suddenly aching sternum. "I get it."

"Deirdre, no. Stop." He blew out air, and she imagined him rubbing his forehead. "What I'm saying is, what if we weren't fake? I've mentioned it before. What if this was real?"

"I—"

"I don't know how to explain this in a way that makes sense. My future has been trapped in my past for a long time. I want to exist in the present." He paused. "Can you be in the present with me, Deirdre?"

Her marriage to Elijah. His death. Her parents' passing. The life she had here in Yukon Valley. The life events she had experienced, and her choices were all like branches on a river, rushing her in sometimes uncontrollable directions.

What if she picked the wrong branch? "Maybe. That's all I can promise. Because of … my past."

"Not the past. I can't compete there—" He cut off her protest. "Not the future either, because thinking about that *will* give me a headache. I only want here and now."

Despite his words, she allowed herself an image of a future that didn't yet exist. A future with Calvin in it. A decision she could trust.

What if she couldn't let go of her fears?

She sat straight up.

What if she *could* let go of her fears?

"I'm not sure," she said, heart hammering and eyes burning. She rubbed her aching chest. "I want to try." Another pause. "I don't want to get hurt."

He breathed once. Twice. Anchoring, calming sounds. A solid structure firmly attached to shore, steadying her in rough emotional waters. "Deirdre, listen. Something I realized after my brain's control-alt-delete is that I need to reach for what I want. Take a risk. No pretending. No lies. No regrets. No hiding my authentic self like I did years ago."

"I understand completely."

"This is my authentic self, saying that he wants to try for a real relationship with your authentic self."

If things worked out, she would be fortunate to have had two men in her life who made her feel special. Guilt popped up before she pushed it back down. "It may not be easy for me."

"Challenging things aren't always easy."

"You've always faced challenges head-on," she murmured.

How could she explain that her heart was at its limit. Any more pain and she would shatter.

"Deirdre, you still there?"

"Yes."

"You don't have to answer right now. I want to do this the right way."

"What do you mean?"

"How about a real date? Not a pretend date."

"Well …"

"Let me try, Deirdre. Let me see if I can be the man I need to be. For you."

You already are. She couldn't make her mouth say the words. "You're a good man."

"I need to be good enough for you."

Chapter Twenty-Seven

DAMN IT ALL, but that Friday evening Cal had a case of the nerves.

Finally, he was back at his rental house, freshly awakened from a hearty afternoon nap, like an exhausted toddler. The constant, dull headache and light sensitivity had receded. Fatigue and fogginess lingered but had improved. Now he understood why patients with head injuries needed time to heal. The injury might not be visible, but it still affected his day-to-day activities.

Thankfully, he had nothing but time right now. No shifts until next week and those would be daytime half-shifts. The chief of staff had accommodated his gradual return to work. Everyone had been great. Especially Deirdre.

They had enjoyed a few more phone calls this week, some steamy enough to get his heart pounding. All of the conversations whetted his appetite for his date with her.

He stepped out of the shower, toweled off, and shaved, careful not to nick himself. No sense bleeding all over her. According to the nurses, he had already done that with his head injury last week when Deirdre had found him at his parents' place.

His hands shook as he buttoned up a gray dress shirt. He

gave up on a necktie. Whether the tremors were due to nerves, fatigue, or brain damage, he refused to venture a guess. At least he was getting better. Hopefully, there would be no permanent damage.

He glanced in the mirror with a barked laugh. It looked like he was going to a business meeting. Which was only funny because this was literally the only business meeting attire he had brought with him. Everything else in the suitcase had been casual clothes, outdoor wear, or scrubs for work.

And two Patagonia vests, of course. You could take the doc out of the ED, but you couldn't take the ED out of the doc.

He caught a glimpse of his graying temples. Time ticked on, regardless of how much he wished otherwise. Hauling in a big breath, he straightened, grabbed a light jacket, and picked up the keychain on the way to his car.

Why did pulling in front of Deirdre's house feel like the eleventh hour before doom? Or the biggest decision of his entire life. He peered at her modest, neat home.

The way he saw it, he had one chance to be the guy he needed to be for her. He had this opportunity to convince Deirdre to stick with him in the near future and maybe more. What about life details? He rubbed his scalp, careful of the healing laceration where the sutures had been removed yesterday.

Thinking about plans and logistics and options made his head hurt again. He'd deal with pesky details about where to live and where to work and what a future meant—later.

Right now, he wanted to focus on Deirdre. No emergencies. No pretending.

Just the actual date night he had always wanted and that she had deserved for far too many years. Years she spent caring for Elijah at the end of his life. Years spent grieving for her parents. Years spent working on the lodge and giving her all to the hospital.

Tonight was hers. Regardless of any future, he would take care of her this evening.

At her front door, he paused before knocking and took a steadying breath.

She opened the door mere seconds after he knocked. "Hi."

Her voice had a breathless quality to it, that Calvin craved to hear right next to his ear. "You look lovely," he said.

She had on a newer pair of hiking boots, leggings, and a V-necked pine-green sweater with sparkly accents near her neck. Gold loop earrings finished out the night-out look.

"You clean up well, yourself."

He shoved a hand in his pocket and waved with the other hand. "Oh, these old rags? *Pshaw.*"

In a matter of seconds, her laugh healed him more than medical care and brain rest ever could. He bent and kissed her on the cheek. It was supposed to be chaste and polite, but damn him if he didn't inhale her floral and fresh linen scent and immediately want to ditch the dinner part of the date and stay in.

"To our fine-dining establishment?" He held out an

elbow and she took it.

The connection and warmth were something he had missed this past week.

"Which place will we be going to this evening?" She knew full well there was only one diner in town.

"That is but one of many surprises for our evening."

Even in the waning twilight, her cheeks glowed pink, and he could have drunk in her beautiful smile for another five minutes.

Opening the car door, he handed her in and came around to the other side. Even though he had been cleared to drive, he remained extra careful. No need to tax his brain with too many hard decisions or multitasking. It was challenging enough thinking straight with the *shushing* fabric sounds and heady scent of her in this confined space.

After parking at the Yukon Valley Diner, he came around again, and she put her hand in his. That small, trusting action made him stand up straighter. Guiding her through the front door, they took a booth near the back.

"Subdued lighting?" she asked with a twinkle in her blue eyes.

"Hey, some of us look better in dim light." He pointed a thumb at his chest. "Truthfully, it's a little easier on my eyes."

"Sure you're okay?" she asked.

"I am now."

They settled in as the waitress poured water and a few minutes later returned to take their orders.

"Thanks for going out with me," he said.

"Of course."

"Not *of course*. You made a choice to be here, after … a lot of things that have happened. That's a big deal."

Her smile belied the vulnerability he glimpsed in her eyes. "What you said about living in the now instead of the past? That kind of hit me in the guilt complex."

"Is that near the liver?"

She shook her head. "Pancreas, I think."

He mock shuddered. "*Oof.* You know the rule. Never mess with the pancreas. It'll flare up if you so much as look at it wrong. Make that organ happy and move the heck on."

She grinned. "You're probably right."

Knocking his knuckles on the table, he said, "So let's circle back to the Breakup Festival."

"Thanks for the topic change. You know, we've already discussed this several times."

"The bonk on the head might have ejected my first year of med school classes, but I still have some ability to read a situation."

She snorted, then clapped her hand over her mouth.

He sat back and appreciated her glowing, lovely, familiar-but-somehow-new-again face. He couldn't process all of the feelings hitting him. The head injury had shaken something loose. Maybe he truly did have more emotional lability after the concussion. It sometimes happened.

Either way, he wrestled control back and concentrated on the conversation. "Festival is tomorrow. Clyde and Amberlyn are leading the gossip charge. The sharks are circling."

"No sharks in the Yukon River. Mostly salmon."

"I meant the hospital staff. The Breakup Festival and dance is all about who you bring, and they're still gunning for us."

Crossing her arms, she said, "I thought they were gunning to win the prediction about when the river ice broke up and the river started flowing."

"Is it flowing yet?"

"The camera that recorded the breakup timed the event at 3:12 a.m. two days ago. Clyde in the ER won the pool this year. Nearly $20,000!"

"Good for him," he said.

"Good for patients and their families. He turned right around and gave half to the hospital foundation to use on resources for family support when patients are hospitalized or in the ED."

"That's awesome. He's a good person."

"His husband would agree, though he's also biased." She grinned. "Clyde's been strutting around, telling everyone about his win."

He chuckled and reached out across the table, relieved when she slid her hand into his. "So. The festival."

"You're like a dog with a bone, aren't you?"

"When I put my mind to something, yes." He rubbed his thumb over the back of her hand, satisfied with her tiny intake of breath. "I'd like to spend Breakup Festival day with you, on another real date."

"We're not even done with this date!" She smiled.

God, what he'd give to see more of that smile.

"I like to plan." He hesitated.

"But?"

"But I'm signed up for the dunking booth to raise money for hospice. Also, I want to honor Elijah."

Her brown eyebrows shot up. "Plunging into ice water doesn't sound safe for you." She motioned toward his head.

"I'm not an invalid. I just had my bell rung."

"Look, I know we use therapeutic hypothermia in certain conditions, but not two weeks after a head injury."

"Eh, won't hurt."

"You sound like your dad."

He palmed his forehead with his free hand. Ouch. Kind of ached. "Never say that again!"

After another minute of gentle laughter, she said, "Tell me a story about growing up with your folks."

"Can do. But only if you'll return the favor with a story about yours."

Her eyes shimmered and he followed the line of her throat as she swallowed.

In a tight voice, she said, "It's a deal."

A few minutes later, their meals arrived, and they dug in. Calvin surprised himself by sharing the story of him and Pop eating all of Mom's blackberries before she could make them into a pie. He had tried to hide the evidence, but the purple all over his face and hands gave away the crime.

"So, Pop didn't get his blackberry pie, I got a bellyache, and Mom refused to fix us any dinner. Those were dark times."

Her sudden sound of mirth surprised both of them, and

she pressed her lips together for a beat. "Sorry."

"Don't be. I love watching you laugh. Glad you find my misery entertaining."

"That's a fun memory."

"It's memorable, all right." He chewed his last bite of salmon patty, then pushed his plate to the side and sat back. "How about you? What's your favorite memory?"

A shadow of a frown came and went as she tapped her lip. "There are a lot to choose from. Things I haven't thought about in a while."

"What was something you and your family enjoyed doing together?"

"Back in the day? Ice fishing, for sure." She leaned forward and dropped her voice. "Not a fan nowadays, obviously."

Right. Her parents' plane crashed, then broke through the ice and into the river. He mentally kicked himself. "Hey. Never mind. You don't have to share. I'm sorry."

"No, it's okay. I mean, there was the one time Mom and Dad took Mav and me backcountry camping for fishing. Dad decided we should all go to a frozen lake way out in the bush. It'd be fun. *Whee.*" She made a twirling motion with her finger. "As a ten-year-old, I was not impressed. Rather stay home and moon over my NSYNC CDs."

"That's fair. Lots of kids thought Justin Timberlake was hot."

"You're not wrong." She shrugged. "So away we went, two sleds, two sets of dogs, ice fishing gear, tents. I'd like to say it was awful, but I really do love the beauty of the landscape here and being outdoors … It was an exciting adventure." She hesitated.

"Until?"

"Until a couple of things happened. Unbeknownst to our parents, Mav and I had eaten all three days' worth of snacks on the ride out." She lifted her hands. "Hey, we were growing kids."

He laced his fingers in hers. He loved how she closed her eyes and beamed, probably envisioning her parents as they had been years ago, healthy and vibrant. "The second thing?"

With a smile, she continued. "Well, one of the younger dogs back then, Naknek, had been chewing on his harness during the run out. We got to the site, and he finally chewed through and escaped to freedom!"

"I thought the dogs were trained to sit down where they stop."

"Not when they are young and excitable. And, as it turns out, not particularly well-suited to dogsledding."

He laughed. "Makes sense."

"When Naknek took off, Dad ran after him, but the teams thought it was a terrific game. They pulled the brake claw out and took off. I was still on Dad's sled. So, it was Dad chasing Naknek followed by me in the cargo basket of a driverless sled being pulled by yapping, ecstatic dogs who had a new game to play. Mom threw Mav back on their sled and took off after us with the dogs on her string, who also thought this was a fun game of chase."

"That had to have been a sight!"

"Oh yeah. My team passed Naknek and Dad within fifty

yards and kept on going. Luckily, I crawled back onto the sled runners to steer and finally slowed down the team. I stomped the claw again and stayed on it until Mom arrived. Thirty minutes later, Dad returned with a dog who felt zero remorse but who had a lot of personal pride. By then, we discovered that Mav and I had eaten through so much food, and at this rate we were at risk of becoming the Donner Party."

He took a mental picture of her happy expression. "What did you do then?"

"Mav started crying because he was already hungry again. Mom walked around talking to herself and making gestures at the sky. Dad fixed Naknek's harness. That dog still had no regrets. After some choice words, Dad turned us back around and home we went." She tilted her head and rested her jaw on a fist. Her eyes took on a wistful glow. "We ended up eating cold sandwiches, popping popcorn, and having a slumber party in the family room. Watched DVDs and laughed all evening."

"I love every bit of that story," he said.

Her smile dropped. "Good memories, for sure." She sighed. "Boy, I miss them."

He pulled her hand to his and pressed it to his cheek for a beat. "Thank you for sharing that with me."

It took her a moment before she said anything. The ever-changing play of emotions over her face fascinated him.

"Thank you for making me remember those times." Her rough voice contained unshed tears.

"I'm honored, Deirdre."

They settled into comfortable silence until the waitress brought the check. After he paid, they strolled back to his car. Once buckled up, the atmosphere inside felt thicker but somehow lighter. He was aware of her every movement. Her every breath.

Arriving back to her home, he kissed her gently on the porch. After a minute, he pulled his head back. "Could I come in?"

"Like, coffee—or more?"

"Whatever you want."

Her shadowed gaze met his. "I want more."

He bent his head and took the kiss deeper, pressing against her. The scorching kiss went on and on until they pulled away, gasping for air.

"Calvin," she panted, fumbling with the key and the doorknob.

"Here, let me. Damn it." He cursed out loud when the key stuck.

His luck. Finally, he wrestled the door open, closed, and he threw the deadbolt.

When he spun back around, Deirdre had turned on the living room lamp, toed off her boots, and started undoing the buttons on his shirt. She froze mid-button and met what he assumed was his mouth-open stare.

"Too fast?" Her chest rose and fell like she had been sprinting.

He snaked an arm around her waist and pressed her against his erection, his breathing equally rapid. "Not fast enough."

Leaning away, he pulled off the shirt then reached for his pants. The thick whiplike sound of his belt leaving the loops was followed by her intake of air. Good. Her pupils dilated in the lamplight. He wanted more of that look. The one where her lips parted, and her eyes went wide.

He closed the distance between them, slid both of his hands around her neck, and cupped the back of her head, drawing her mouth to his.

With her fingers, she traced his neck and gripped the hair at the nape, blasting all coherent thought from his mind. When he took another break from his kisses, her face shone up at him, lips glistening. He bent and ran the tip of his tongue over her upper lip.

"God, I want you, Deirdre."

"You have me."

He wanted to ask, *all of you*?

The answer didn't matter. He was the right guy for the right woman, right now. That was enough.

Dropping down for another kiss, he licked and nipped his way over her neck then back to her lips until her sighs caused an acute reaction in his pelvis. He reached down to adjust his pants. Didn't help.

The only thing that would cure what ailed him was her trembling and moaning in his arms as she went to blissful pieces.

She drifted her hands over his bare abdomen, drawing shudders and testing his control.

Slowly walking her back to the bedroom while kissing her and discarding clothes along the way, Calvin paused to enjoy the vision of Deirdre. Her hair tousled, sweater off and bra straps sliding down her arms. Yes. More of this. He flipped on the bedside lamp.

She put a hand on his heaving chest and winked at him. "Oh, does this count as exertion? Because the doctor said to avoid that."

He unhooked her bra and tossed it on the floor. "Well, I'm something of a medical professional myself and therefore can provide an objective second opinion." He cupped her breast and ran a thumb over the taut tip.

Panting, she said, "I don't want to be the cause of more damage to your head."

"My … head … will be damaged if you're not naked, *stat*."

The laugh erupting from her morphed into a keening sound of pleasure as he bent and drew the nipple into his mouth, carefully scraping his teeth over the sensitive flesh.

"Oh my God," she breathed, tightening her hand on the back of his neck.

After treating the other breast to similar care because he didn't play favorites, he took her hand and guided her down to the bed.

Chapter Twenty-Eight

"ARE YOU GOOD?" Calvin lifted his head from where he had been busy tormenting her sensitive breasts until she squirmed.

"Very good," she gasped. "You?"

"I could be better."

Her sentences had gotten much shorter. Seemed her own brain wasn't functioning at 100 percent. "Oh?" she asked. Maybe his head injury was causing him issues.

He twirled his tongue over her tight nipple, then lifted his head. "You could be naked."

"Hey, fair's fair, buddy." She pointed at him.

Calvin shucked his pants in a millisecond and then ran his fingertips under the waistband of her leggings. "If you don't mind laying back, that will help me to not exert myself too much."

Laughing, she complied, and her hips bucked with the force of him whipping off her leggings and socks. He paused. Waited. Licked his lips. Stared down at her.

Waited some more.

"Oh my gosh. Come here now!" she insisted, reaching for him.

He remained out of reach, biting his thumb as he gazed

over her, his eyes darkened.

Her limbs were askew on the bed, legs splayed. Deirdre had no desire to hide from him. She trusted Calvin.

Always had.

His low voice sent chills over her hypersensitive nerves. "This last week, I missed you. I missed this. I almost missed so much more." He crawled toward her on the bed, easing her legs open with his knees and pressing his warm palm against her mound. "When I think about what I almost lost. What I almost never had."

She groaned. "How about what you're not going to get if you don't hurry up."

He pulled his head back. "Are you giving me an order?"

"You're off the clock." She strained her hips toward him, but he held her still. "Yes." She gasped. "That's an order."

With a shake of his head, he shrugged. "My concussion makes it hard to compute."

Sitting straight up, she leaned forward and wrapped her hand around his erect penis. "Feeling cognitively intact now?"

"Alert and oriented," he said between a clamped jaw. "Damn it. You're killing me." He rocked into her hand.

"Good." She squeezed gently until his eyes rolled back. "You. Me. Now."

"Yes, ma'am."

They tumbled back on the bed together, Calvin bracketing her body with his long arms and legs in the most sensual of prisons. He slowly flexed his torso, and they groaned together at the hot skin-to-skin friction. It wasn't enough.

She was still incomplete.

He reached down to cup her pulsing, hot flesh and she ground against his hand, frantic to relieve the building pressure. Foreplay was fine, but tonight she craved immediate connection. Reassurance that he was here, with her.

"Calvin."

In a flash, he stood and sheathed himself with a condom, then knelt again, teasing her entrance and spreading her wet arousal over his tip. She squirmed, needing him inside of her.

He slid home in one long, slow move. Then he held still, filling her completely. Not moving his hips but simply remaining connected deep inside of her, he cupped his hands around her head, kissing her deeply. The strokes of his tongue filled her, mirroring how he completed her elsewhere. Her nerves quivered. Every muscle tensed and released, chasing more friction and movement.

She gripped his forearms and held on tight.

He was so real. So alive. So much a part of her heart and body.

With another deep kiss, he growled and flexed his hips in strong, looping movements.

Every controlled but relentless stroke drove him deeper into her. Filled her in a way she had never quite experienced before.

She gazed up at him in the brief moments when he lifted his head to breathe between kisses. His intense gray gaze met hers.

"Deirdre, this is—I—" He sounded as if the words were ripped out of him.

Lifting her head to kiss him, she gasped. "I know. You're—oh, God."

At the end of each stroke, he ground against her, lighting up nerve endings. Pushing her higher and higher.

"Calvin." She pulled him tightly against her and lifted her ankles to his hips.

He groaned with each thrust, and she echoed him, their cries rising until she exploded around him with a soul-deep climax that went on and on.

"Deirdre!" He followed her over the edge, driving with short, hard movements that amplified her body's responses.

After what felt like several minutes, they both stilled, breathing harshly, arms wrapped tightly around one another. Still connected, they pulsed together as aftershocks rippled through them. Sweat cooled on their skin.

Cal's lips pressed against her neck. "I could get used to this," he said.

She ran her hands over his lean back. "I don't want this to end." The truth stunned her.

She wasn't just describing their physical connection.

When he eased away and slid out of her, they both groaned. Her hypersensitive nerves wanted more.

Her heart wanted more.

"I don't want this to end, either." His low chuckle rumbled through her. "Give me five, maybe ten minutes, and I should be good to go again with that light exertion."

Chapter Twenty-Nine

T HE NEXT MORNING, Deirdre slowly opened her eyes. Sunlight streamed into the bedroom where the blinds hadn't been completely closed last night.

Last night, they had turned into each other's arms to sleep. She studied the relaxed expression on Calvin's face.

He was alive. Safe. Healthy.

Wow, healthy indeed.

Last night was amazing, of course. Several times they had connected in tangles of kisses and limbs.

Letting go of residual fears had left her feeling closer to him but also raw and vulnerable.

She couldn't stop to dwell on the what-ifs of life's uncertainties down the road.

Like how normal relationships worked.

She closed her eyes. *Normal relationships.*

Trust. Hope. Communication.

Living in the present without being paralyzed by the past or the future. That was what Deirdre wanted.

When she opened her eyes, Calvin was watching her with a thoughtful expression in his gray eyes. Eyes that she could fall into over and over again.

"Morning," he said as he planted a kiss on her forehead.

Somehow that action, with them in bed with mere inches separating them, was as intimate as what they had done last night.

"Good morning," she murmured.

Deirdre snuggled into the warmth of the bed and his body, tucking her cheek against his chest. She inhaled his scent of aftershave and warm, sexy male.

He tugged the blanket up and smoothed a hand over her shoulder. "Big day today."

Her heart thudded. Why?

At her expression, he added, "Breakup Festival. Dunk for hospice. Icy plunge for dollars?"

"Mmm. Yep."

In unison, they both stretched and rubbed against each other with twin whimpers at the warm, sensual friction.

A minute later, he sat up and winced slightly when his face intersected the beam of dawn light.

"You okay?"

"Bright sunshine still takes some adjustment." He raised a hand to block the light. "I'm good."

She hopped out of bed and closed the blinds. "Think coffee will help?"

"How could it not? Does it come with anything else, like bacon or eggs?" He held his arms out to her, and she tumbled into his embrace.

"I can see what the chef can whip up." She laughed.

He wrapped her in his arms and planted a kiss on her neck, his lips drifting to her breasts. Then he glided a hand over her abdomen, teasing even lower, and said, "A different kind of breakfast could be better."

After a few more kisses and toe-tingling licks, she swatted him. "Hey, we have work to do today. Charity. Dating. Working the hospital event. Assorted tomfoolery. There's a schedule to keep."

"You're good at flipping into admin mode."

"Is that bad?"

"It's accurate."

"Fair enough."

After showering, they slipped on clothes that had to be retrieved from various locations in the house. Then they enjoyed a nice breakfast together, punctuated by little touches and the occasional heated kiss.

With a dark frown, Calvin glanced at his buzzing phone.

"Anything going on?" she said, not trying to pry.

He blinked. The expression shifted to a carefully neutral look. "Nope." His voice remained rock-steady. "Need to take care of something quick before the festival. No big deal."

"Can I help?"

"You can come here for a few more seconds." Then Calvin pulled her onto his lap and kissed her one more time.

A few minutes later, he left the house to go get ready for the day.

At noon, in her boots, leggings, long-sleeve thermal shirt and a Yukon Valley Hospital-branded pine green jacket, she left the house. She headed toward the Yukon Valley Fairgrounds, otherwise known as the high school-middle school-elementary school parking lot and adjacent sports field. The event overlooked the river, which, true enough, now flowed downstream, a few straggling ice pieces chasing their way toward the Bering Sea.

The weather, always iffy in mid-April, had hung in there today. It was cool in the fifties, and cloudy skies held back the precipitation so far. Colorful balloons and decorations brightened the ticket booth. Local vendors sold crafts and food. Feats of skill attracted gaggles of children and teenagers, eager to win prizes and impress their friends.

"Hi, Dee," Mav called out to her. He and Dr. Tipton—Lee—strolled up, hand in hand.

"You both off duty today?" Deirdre said.

"Yes, and our weekend guests are somewhere in the crowd, enjoying the festivities. So, no lodge work this afternoon. We get to have a day out together." He hugged Lee to his side and they both shared a warm smile that sent a cascade of emotions through Deirdre.

In the end, she was happy her little brother had found someone he loved and who loved him in return. Despite Lee's petite frame and Mav's tall bulk, they fit perfectly together.

"You here solo?" he asked, a glint in his eye.

"Real suave, Mav." She glanced around. "I'm looking for the hospital dunking booth."

"You volunteering?" His brows drew together as he studied her.

Mav knew why there was no way would Deirdre ever set foot in a device meant to throw her into ice-laden water. An acidic wave of panic climbed her throat at the mere thought.

"No. Calvin's supposed to take a turn."

Lee's blonde eyebrows shot up. "Um. Huh."

Then she quickly clamped her mouth together but made a slashing motion with her hand. As Calvin's treating physician, she hadn't spilled any information, but it was obvious her opinion of his choice of activity.

Deirdre nodded. "*Um* is right. That's exactly what I told him. Don't worry. I'll sort it out."

"I bet you will," Mav mumbled. "Speaking of reasons why he shouldn't risk worsening his head injury, is Calvin doing okay? Unofficially speaking." He lifted a hand in an aside to Lee. "She and Calvin were on a date last night. News travels fast. I'm not breaching HIPAA here."

Lee's bright laugh caught Mav's attention, and he grinned down at her, obviously smitten.

How was Calvin doing? Deirdre knew exactly how he was doing. How every … inch … of him was doing. Seemed healthy to her.

"He's well." She gulped. "Any word from those jerks who hurt Calvin?"

"Nothing. Radio silence. Not even the Alaska state troopers can find them." Mav tightened his arm around Lee. "Which is good and bad."

"I hear what you're saying," Deirdre said. "We'll have to let law enforcement keep working the case." She paused as she scanned the event. "Oh, looks like I'm heading over"— she caught sight of several pine-green jacketed participants in a cluster—"thataway."

"See you later, sis."

Deirdre wove through the crowd. Every year, all of Yukon Valley as well as the people living in the surrounding villages and homesteads came out to enjoy the unique Breakup Festival. There was a Breakup queen and king contest, as well as a Breakup dance later tonight.

All of the food and drink incorporated the theme of ice, down to the iced cookies and various flavors of icebox pies. Every booth activity had a link to the river or ice as well.

As she approached the Yukon Valley Hospital's dunk for hospice tank, she laughed as teenagers spurred each other on.

In one booth was Dr. Burmeister, in a wetsuit—smart guy. He was blowing raspberries and making moose ears at the kids while his legs swung from his perch on the platform.

"I delivered some of you people, and I coach the rest of you in basketball. I can't believe this level of disrespect!" He made his eyes bug out. "I've even seen some of you naked!"

The kids roared and hurled balls in manufactured ire, all missing the bull's-eye in the middle of the bright yellow canvas flap. When the children turned around, hopping up and down and pleading, their parents handed over more tickets so the kids could reload.

In the other booth was Anna Smits, the hospital CEO, who appeared to be in a thermal underwear top over a jog-bra, a crinoline tutu, and a giant sparkly tiara. She also worked the crowd. "Folks, my booth time is ticking down. Hospital staff, now's your chance. You know you've always wanted to dunk on the CEO! It's for a good cause!"

Jeff Johns, the aging CFO, gamely stepped up, dropped a bunch of tickets in the bucket, and threw. One ball hit the target but didn't move the lever.

"No fair!" He pointed.

"You have to be accurate *and* have power, Jeff. Pencil pushing did not prepare you for this challenge!" Anna egged him on.

He wound up again and hurled a few more balls, finally moving the lever with a loud *clang* of the bell. Anna dropped into the water with a big splash. The crowd cheered.

Deirdre held her midsection but wasn't laughing. She couldn't breathe. The flashbacks to her parents' icy deaths didn't get better with each passing year of the dunk for hospice. Logically, Deirdre knew it was not the same. She knew.

But the thought of the fall into frigid water. The inability to breathe. It literally swamped her.

Anna emerged, laughing and gasping as an attendant pulled her out, wrapped her in a blanket, and helped her to the warming tent.

Deirdre faked enthusiasm as she clapped and chatted with several hospital staff and families nearby.

Jeff swaggered and high-fived the teenagers.

The kids redoubled their efforts until Dr. Burmeister hit the water after a *clang*.

Behind the booth and off to the side, she spied Calvin, peeking out from the tent. Her heart melted like the ice in the river.

He winced in the light and shaded his eyes with a hand.

The brightness had to hurt with the constant lingering headache. Yet he appeared prepared to keep his assignment for the hospice booth.

The hospice team had supported Deirdre through Elijah's end-of-life care. Hospice brought comfort to so many patients and families at the most difficult time in their lives.

Even despite not feeling 100 percent, Calvin was going to fulfill his promise. Raise money. Honor Elijah.

Take a risk, albeit a small one. Accept discomfort in doing so.

She looked at the tank, then to Calvin.

Something in her heart cracked open a tiny bit. Grief persisted, but her heart had grown large enough to fit more. So much more.

"Calvin, wait," she called out as she hurried over.

His brows shot up and he smiled with a pained squint of one eye. "Nice day for a swim, huh?" He observed the tank dubiously.

"No. I'm taking your place."

"What?"

She urged him back into the warming tent where Anna Smits and Dr. Burmeister toweled off. Deirdre started shucking layers down to her leggings and thermal top. "Anna, can I borrow your water shoes?"

"Good luck!" The CEO handed them over.

"Deirdre, I know what it is for you to do this." Calvin's voice pitched low. He steadied her by an arm as she slipped on the cold, wet shoes in the cool air. "Stop. You don't have to get in the booth."

"No. It's not safe for you with the head injury. I know you cared about Elijah. He was your best friend. I know that you want to raise money for hospice. But this isn't safe. I'll take your turn."

His brows dropped. "Sitting in icy water is the very least I can do to honor Elijah's life."

"No question. I know that, and I'm sure Elijah knows it, too." She smiled as she recalled the time they had spent together years ago as teenagers. The vitality they all had. The friendship and joy. "It's the least I can do, as well. For Elijah."

The corners of his mouth tightened.

"For me." She added, "And for you."

"You're one amazing woman." He brushed a kiss over her forehead.

She didn't care that her colleagues' eyes popped open. No more hiding her heart.

"I'm about to be a chilly woman, but for a good cause."

Calvin drew on pants and a fleece over his own bike shorts and T-shirt.

No lie, he would have looked great up there in the booth.

He grinned when he caught her staring. "Okay, popsicle time." He held open the tent flap.

The hospice team cheered as Deirdre waved to the on-lookers with confidence she did not feel as she walked the ten or so feet from the tent to the tank. Gripping the handrails, she put her foot on the bottom rung of the tank ladder and froze.

"You've got this," Calvin said from right behind her. "I'm going to stay right here."

Her heart hammered and cold air burned her lungs.

Her hands shook as she climbed the ladder. It was a dunk tank, not a frozen river. Her logical brain knew that. Even as she slowly scooted out on the platform and peered down into the ice pieces bobbing in the water, she envisioned her parents' last moments. Her eyes burned.

"Go, Dee!" Mav called out.

She met his eyes, and he nodded. He knew what this cost her. Their parents' death had cost them both.

It was past time for a new start. A reset. She was ready to experience a springtime that held hope instead of fear.

Bundled in her fleece jacket and with a beanie over her wet hair, Anna took over barker duties with a wave of her hands. "All right, folks. By special appearance, we've got Yukon Valley Hospital's chief nursing officer, Deirdre Steen. For the next fifteen minutes, this is your chance." She closed one eye and peered at Deirdre. "Who's tired of AIDET training? Sick of never-ending policy updates? Here's your chance to get those feelings out of your system before you have to do more annual training modules!"

Hospital staff fake-booed, then everyone laughed together. Deirdre peered out at the crowd. Friends and coworkers gathered, smiling and shouting encouragement. Butch and Aggie joined the group and waved. Mav and Lee cheered. A swell of happy community support flowed around Deirdre.

Amberlyn ponied up some tickets and threw the balls halfheartedly.

"You can do better than that!" Deirdre called out, secretly glad that the nurse missed the target.

"I don't want to add a hypothermic patient to the ED

census!" Amberlyn shouted back.

Deirdre swung her legs, feet not quite touching the water. "Is no one brave enough to risk my wrath?"

Tuli, leaning on a cane, stepped up. Where had he come from? The crowd had really grown. He handed a wad of tickets and glanced over at Louise, who stood near her parents and her bundled-up brother Gordy who grinned from a wheelchair. After leaning his cane against the chair and giving Gordy a fist bump, Tuli made a big show of warming up his throwing arm. "This is for all of those seven a.m. meetings!" He lifted his arms, urging the crowd to cheer louder.

Deirdre stuck her tongue out at Tuli but eyed the water warily. She glanced at the digital clock to the side of the tank. She had ten more minutes. What were the chances she would escape dry?

Tuli tossed the ball up and caught it a few times with the obvious skill of someone who had played baseball and the showmanship of a former team captain. He cocked his arm back, but Dr. Burmeister emerged from the tent and stopped him.

"Ah, ah, ah. Former state champions have to stand back farther," he said.

"Aww," the crowd mumbled.

Tuli shook his head and limped back another ten feet as indicated. Then he turned toward the crowd. "Hey, folks, do we want this to go viral for a good cause?"

Everyone cheered as Tuli pulled out his phone and hit a few buttons. Handing the phone to Lee, he posed, then spoke into the camera. "A warm welcome coming to you live from Yukon Valley's world-famous Breakup Festival. We're here at Yukon Valley Hospital's dunk for hospice. Don't forget to like and share my video to support this good cause! Now, let's see if the best pitching arm in Yukon Valley High School history can still do the job." He squared up on the arbitrary line Dr. Burmeister had drawn.

First throw—wide.

Some people heckled; others groaned.

Deirdre unclenched her hands from the thin metal seat and took a deep breath.

Dr. Burmeister goaded him. "State champion? What position did you play? Statistician?"

Everyone laughed.

Calvin cheered along behind her. "You've got this, Deirdre! Show him who's boss. Literally."

Tuli peered at the target and wound up.

The ball glanced off the target but did not activate it.

It was hard to hear the shouts of the crowd over the hammering of her heart. One more ball to go and she might be safe.

Lee held up the phone and panned from the booth back to Tuli.

"Hey, hey. I missed on purpose with that last one. A false sense of security," Tuli said with a cheeky grin. He winked. "Right, Lou?"

The EMT blushed crimson.

Once again Tuli wound up and fired.

Clang!

The seat dropped out from under Deirdre, her stomach following.

In an instant, ice and water surrounded her, frigid and heavy, stealing her breath, compressing her lungs. Was this what it felt like for her parents, still in the plane and deep in the river? Not able to breathe. Frozen.

She splashed, then stood up, her head breaking the surface, small bits of ice floating nearby. "So cold!" She gasped.

She was alive.

Breathing.

For some reason, she wanted to both laugh and cry.

She had not felt this alive in so long. Almost like her soul had been hibernating for years. Finally, in the fresh air and the promise of spring renewal, she had emerged.

The cheers faded into a dull roar, like her head was in a small barrel. Epiphany over. She'd overcome a huge fear, and she needed out of the tank. Now.

"I've got you." Calvin's mellow voice calmed her as he reached into the tank and grasped her arms.

Chapter Thirty

CAL WRAPPED HER in a big flannel blanket. What had taking his place cost her?

"You did a great job." Unable to stop himself, he dropped his head for a kiss, alarmed at how cold her lips were. He pulled the blanket closer around her and chafed his hands up and down her shivering back.

"I can't believe we did that. Here. In front of everyone," she said.

He pulled back. "Kissing? Are you okay with it?" he asked.

She tucked her head into his neck and burrowed into the blanket. "Depends."

"On what?"

"What it means."

The time was now. Cal cleared his throat and leaned back. "It means that I—"

A booming voice cut through the noise. "Is this what you bumpkins do for fun?" Randy strode through the crowd, hitting Lee's shoulder and knocking her off-balance.

Two other people followed him. Cal's gut dropped to the temperature of that damned dunk tank. His head throbbed. He recognized the other two people from the attack at his parents' place.

Right on time. He scanned the crowd. No. Not yet.

Maverick yanked Lee to his side and wrapped an arm around her shoulders. Then he bared his teeth. "Folks have been looking for you. Friend."

Cal tightened his hold around Deirdre and rotated so they were sideways to the newcomers. Randy and his friends would have to come through Cal if they wanted to touch her.

"When I'm done with this town, you'll all be working for me." Randy sneered.

"Not likely," Maverick said.

"So you think." Randy strolled up to Cal and pulled out folded paper from his coat pocket. "Here it is, like we agreed. I have the check and the paperwork to sign over the property. No one else has to get hurt."

"What?" Deirdre gasped.

In his peripheral vision, Cal spied the twin slack-jawed expressions of Mom and Pop, along with others in the crowd that had grown dead silent. Cal kept his arm around a gaping Deirdre. The color rose in her face, turning her into a spitting-mad Deirdre.

He squeezed her shoulder, hoping she'd trust him. "So, you want me to hand over the family's homestead so you can dig up our mountains and ruin our town."

"What's there to ruin? It's already backward here. Look around." He lifted his hand to somehow encompass the colorful decorations, craft vendors, and community service booths. "Besides, we had a deal."

Cal pivoted to keep Randy and his friends in his sights and protect Deirdre. He also needed to keep Randy talking for a few more minutes. "Why aren't you giving this deal to the other property owners? To the corporation?"

"Corporation?" Randy laughed. "Oh, you mean the *Indian tribe*?"

Tuli's dark expression was mirrored by other native Alaskans present. He took his phone back from Lee and turned it on Randy.

"I only need one point of entry to access the range." Randy waved the check. "You said that your parents would be out of here soon. Less to deal with. You're gone soon, too, right? This money will pay for you all to take a nice vacation." Sniffing, he scowled at the gray skies. "Not here, though."

Pop glowered.

Mom's mouth dropped open. "Calvin?" she said.

"Calvin?" Deirdre said pushing away from him, still shivering.

Silence fell all around him.

His head pounded. This town and these people were his home.

Randy said again, "We had a deal."

Cal glanced down at Deirdre, her wet hair and droplets in her eyelashes making him want to warm her inside and out. This woman was his home. He would do anything to remove the shock and disappointment on her face.

"Is this true?" she asked.

"Sure is," Randy said.

Maverick took a step forward. "You. Shut it."

Randy snorted as his two partners closed ranks with him.

Everyone believed Cal had betrayed his parents and the entire town. So be it. "He's right. We did have a deal."

No one moved in the crowd.

Randy sneered and lifted his chin.

"How could you do something like this?" Deirdre's words fell like physical slaps against his face.

She pushed back against him, but he didn't fully let go. Not yet. He shifted so she stood next to him, his arm draped over her shoulders.

Cal blew out a breath and fought to remain calm and take his time. "It's true. I met with Randy recently, hoping to understand what it was he wanted and to see if there was a way to work together. Before that, I had come back to Yukon Valley to encourage my parents to move to a bigger town where there were more services for their health. Where it wouldn't be so difficult for them to keep up with their property. Where they'd be safer than in Yukon Valley."

"Son," Pop said. "That's low."

Lifting his hands as if he could hold back the waves of disappointment coming from his friends and family, Cal swallowed a hard lump and said, "You're right, Pop. Doesn't matter that I only did it because I wanted what's best for you and Mom. It was a low thing to do."

Deirdre's blue eyes pinned him in place. "So, when I saw with you and Randy in the diner? You really were meeting with him and making a deal."

"Yes, he was," Randy said.

Right as Cal said, "No."

Randy pulled his chin back. "It's all right here." He held out the envelope.

Cal killed a little more time while he planted his feet shoulder-width apart and put his free hand on his hip. "Here's my final offer. You and your investors can go to hell. Good luck ruining another town."

"You said that you didn't care about this one-horse town," the guy growled. "Said you might as well make a buck from it." Randy's eyes shifted as he stepped back.

With subtle movements, the crowd formed a semi-circle around him. Randy and his friends were going nowhere.

Cal lifted his chin. "That's what you thought I said. What you wanted to hear." He sniffed. "As far as I'm aware, Yukon Valley and the land around it are not for sale. At least not by me. This is my family and friends you're talking about. People I care about. You're not going to terrorize anyone else."

Randy and his two friends took threatening steps toward Cal, but the sheer mass of pissed-off people surrounding them checked their movements.

"We had a deal," Randy said. "We shook on it. You signed a paper."

"Did we now? Sorry, can't recall. My head injury caused memory loss."

"You're going to regret this," Randy yelled over the grumbles of the angry crowd.

"I regret talking with you in the first place. Look, I made a mistake in thinking there could be some scenario where everyone benefits from working together. You've made it clear that's not possible."

"The contract! It's right here!" Randy yelled.

Mom put her hands over her mouth. Pop glared holes into both Randy and Cal. The crowd waited.

Deirdre's sharp gasp next to him scared him more than all of the other reactions combined.

Calmer than he had ever been in his life, Cal said, "See, here's the problem, friend. I can't sign over something that isn't mine to give. Even if you have something with my signature on it, the paper is worthless."

Randy's face turned beet red. "What?" The envelope crumpled in his fist. "You said your folks weren't making decisions anymore, that you were the legal power of attorney."

"Did I give you that impression? Huh, guess I made a mistake there, too."

Pop kept his eyes on Randy as he strode ten paces to where Cal stood. "As you can see, I have no problems making decisions here. Aggie, honey, how about you?"

Mom joined them, mad as a hornet, nearly vibrating, and whipped around to face Randy, whose red face turned white. For a second, Cal worried about Randy's wellbeing. Pop snaked an arm around her waist, ostensibly affectionate but more keeping her from killing the speculator.

"Decisions are no problem for me. I feel completely clearheaded. Too clear, in fact," she said.

"But our meeting today." Randy whipped his head around. "You made me come out here to finalize the deal."

Deirdre pressed her shoulder more firmly to Cal's side. His heart swelled at her lifted chin and blue glint as she glared lasers at Randy.

"I got tired of you insulting and hurting people and the town I care about," Cal said. "You had gone to ground, and the only thing that would flush you out was your greed."

"But—"

"Lieutenant Kate? Are you here?" Cal shouted.

"I'm on it," the trooper said with a tip of her navy-blue hat as she stepped through the back of the crowd.

The lieutenant and three troopers—the sum total of Yukon Valley's Alaska state trooper detachment—emerged from their positions behind the warming tent and from the next booth over. With big, friendly Yukon Valley smiles, the troopers rescued Randy and his friends from the swarming mad spectators that had trapped them.

Kate was all business. "I don't get to do this very much in our 'one-horse town,' but today I'm going to read your rights, sir. You are being arrested for attempted murder, conspiracy to murder, intent to defraud, and criminal trespass."

"Murder? No." Randy's face turned red as he pointed. "Hey, I didn't hit him. Jacob did."

Kate's expression could generously be described as unimpressed. "You planned it. But sure, maybe Jacob will testify that this was all his idea and get you off the hook."

Jacob, now in cuffs, sputtered and denied that accusation.

The lieutenant's tight smile would make the most crooked criminal walk a straight line. "You're done terrorizing the fine people of this town." She paused and the click of his handcuffs echoed loud in the dead silence. "Take them away." Then she high-fived a nearby teenager whose mouth gaped open and eyes were huge. "I always wanted to say that."

Randy, his friends, and the three troopers left.

Lieutenant Kate turned to the kids gathered around her. With a wry expression and a shrug, she started answering their chattered, rapid-fire questions about being an Alaska state trooper.

Mom and Pop faced Cal.

Maverick and Lee walked over to him.

He loved his family and Deirdre's, but he truly cared about the woman in his arms and wanted to get her warmed up and clear the air between them.

"Calvin?" Deirdre looked up at him. If he could memorize that beautiful awestruck expression, he'd be a lucky man. "What did you do?"

"I wanted to be a good enough man for you."

"But—"

He raised a finger. "Wait. I need to say my piece. Randy was partially right about some of it. I made some mistakes. However, I realized some important things over this past month, and I promised myself that I'd fix my errors."

"I can't believe you baited Randy into showing his face here."

"Greed is that guy's catnip. He couldn't resist the chance of closing the deal."

"I'm sorry I jumped to conclusions when I saw you meeting with him."

"You weren't exactly wrong, Deirdre." He dropped his hands on her blanket-covered shoulders, and he hauled in a shaky breath. "I made other mistakes. With you."

She studied him for a beat. "We both did."

"Listen, I can't fight a ghost."

"I never asked you to," she said. "Never once."

"I know that. It was me. I was the one fighting to be better than your best memories of Elijah. Now I realize that it doesn't matter. We can both love Elijah and remember his life. I finally got it through my hard head that I measure up on my own."

"Calvin." Her eyes turned watery. "What are you saying?"

"I want to be the man for you. Not in the past. In the present. I want to be the right man, right now, and maybe for years to come. What do you say?"

The blanket fell to the ground as she kissed him.

Chapter Thirty-One

DEIRDRE CLOSED THE few inches between them and kissed Calvin, loving the feel of his firm lips on hers. The familiar scent of him. His strong arms around her.

After a minute, she pulled her head back, breathless. "It was never a competition, you know. I loved Elijah. True. But I-I love you, as well. You are two amazing men. Two different men. Two different times. Two different Deirdres."

His eyes shimmered. "You love me?" he said.

"Absolutely. My heart wants you, Calvin." She kissed him again, then drew back. "What about your future? Your plans? Are you thinking here? Seattle? Or—"

"As long as I'm with you, that's a future I can look forward to." With his thumb, he brushed a tear from her cheek. "I love you with everything that I am, Deirdre. You have no idea. If I'm lucky, you'll let me try and show you." He kissed her as everyone around them cheered.

Out of the corner of her eye, she spied Mav and Lee hugging each other. Aggie rested her head on Bruce's shoulder. The Smith family, including a smiling Gordy, all clappeed.

Tuli waved at the crowd, phone still raised and recording. "Yoohoo! Don't I get a prize for raising funds for hospice *and* getting these two kids together?"

"How do you figure all of that?" Bruce groused as he turned around.

"They bonded in the ED over my leg, which got the ball rolling. Then I dunked Deirdre and Calvin rescued her. When he was feeling all pumped up, he sacked the bad guy. Now he's riding a high filled with success and love. To think it all started right here." He patted his chest. Tuli actually strutted a few steps until he winced as he stumbled with his bum leg. Retrieving the cane that Louise handed him, he huffed, "Once again, I get no credit." He planted his cane firmly in the ground, muttering to anyone that would listen.

Calvin laughed, then sobered as he looked around at family and friends. "Everyone, we also need to come clean about the dating situation."

"Oh. *Ohh*," Deirdre said. "That's right. They don't know."

"We have to confess to another crime," he said. "We were pretending to date so you all would stop bugging us."

No one said anything, until everyone burst out laughing.

"Good one, Calvin. We all knew the truth because we have eyeballs and brain cells." Mav grinned. "You two are terrible at pretending."

Lee chimed in, "Hopefully, you two peas in a pod are better at treating patients and writing hospital policy than you are at fake dating."

"What?" Deirdre asked.

Aggie patted her on the arm. "It was kind of obvious all along."

"We didn't fool anyone?" Cal said.

Tuli raised his dark eyebrows and pressed a hand to his chest. "I totally bought it."

Deirdre said, "Really?"

He laughed. "Nope. Even in meetings, you couldn't stop from shooting each other googly eyes."

"Oh man," she said.

Cal turned her so she faced him, keeping his hands on her shoulders. He couldn't bring himself to lose physical connection with her. "So, Deirdre Steen, here's the question. Are you willing to continue fake dating me? Maybe for years to come?"

Deirdre threw her arms around him. "I would fake date you forever." After another long kiss, she shivered. "Could you toss that blanket back over me? It's freezing out here in Alaska."

The End

Author Notes

If you enjoyed this book, would you consider leaving a review and letting others know about the story? This helps authors more than you may realize.

Please feel free to follow me at jilliandavid.net/newsletter-signup.html to get the insider info on all of my shenanigans – both medical and authorly!

For friends and family who have recently discovered I write romance novels: *this book is fiction, people.* I promise, it's made up.

That said, I put so many medical Easter eggs and insider jokes in this book. I hope you enjoy finding them all! Recall that I'm a rural doctor who has only practiced medicine in remote towns with fewer than three stoplights. I've also enjoyed years as a physician leader, so my insider administrator information is solid!

Here are a couple of truths about this book:

Press-Ganey scores are a thing. Docs kind of hate them. Patients are given a survey to fill out after their visit, and these scores get reviewed by the employer and then published. Oftentimes, patients score things out of our control, like the type of muffins served on the breakfast tray—no joke, that complaint yielded a one-star review—which is super frustrating. Sometimes, patients get mad we didn't give them an addictive or dangerous medication or run an unnecessary test, and so they vent on those forms. Good times. While I've been fortunate to have high scores, I take the results with a grain of salt.

There is data to support an interesting paradox. The patients who are the most satisfied on these surveys have, percentage-wise, the highest iatrogenic morbidity and mortality. What does that mean? Medical professionals understand that treatments which could make patients very happy—medications with significant risks, unnecessary and invasive procedures or tests, for example—can also increase the risk of complications, side effects, other health issues, and, well, *death*. In short, the most satisfied patients—based on these types of scores—also are the most healthcare injured or dead. It's wild. Sadly, some medical systems still pressure healthcare workers to try to get the scores high, which puts the focus on patient satisfaction instead of patient safety.

AIDET training. Ugh. There are myriad patient communication-patient satisfaction techniques we have been subjected to over the years. AIDET, BATHE technique, OARS communication tools, Horty Springer, and the list goes on. Sometimes these methods feel cringe-worthy, but for healthcare workers who may not possess the innate ability to clearly communicate with other human beings—looking at you, ortho! (Okay, fine. Not all ortho folks.)—these tools can be helpful.

Annual training modules. They suck. They are supposed to take multiple hours to do. I can complete mine way faster than that. Don't tell anyone, but I generally hit play on the module and then go see some patients, return and hit play again, and repeat until done.

Yes, I have seen polar plunges for hospice where a big chunk of ice was cut out of the frozen lake and rescue divers in drysuits deployed, so that docs and nurses and anyone else can take a chilly dip to raise funds for hospice and still survive. The most disturbing plunge for hospice image burned into my retinas is a picture forever enshrined in the local newspaper. Our very hairy general surgeon was caught on film leaping in midair above the opening in the icy lake in ten-degree temps, wearing nothing but a coconut shell bikini and a grass hula skirt. He raised something like $5000. I'm guessing the donations were as much for hospice as they were to deter him from ever wearing that outfit again.

Ray Mountains ores and rare earth elements? That's kind of a thing. Apparently even a blind squirrel sometimes finds a nut, and that was me stumbling into mineral research on a mountain range that I randomly selected in book one. Go, me! Now I know all about the industrial applications of rare earth elements.

Blending professional and personal lives in rural areas can be tricky. Hoo boy, this has been a challenge during my career. I've had patients approach me for medical advice while I'm out to dinner with family. Hubs was cool with it until one lady started describing a rather ... personal ... problem in front of him. While he was trying to eat his appetizer. The graphic details involved both color and scent. Yikes.

I've gotten better about directing patients to make an appointment so I can properly—and medicolegally—help them.

Boundaries with my coworkers. If a doc hangs with the same OR-ED-nursing crew long enough, and it's like having work siblings who are very comfortable and have zero problem asking some borderline inappropriate questions from time to time!

Boundaries, part 2. If you're the new doc in a town of under 5,000 population, it is my experience that people you've never met will know 1) where you're from, 2) how you ended up here, 3) what your marital status is, 4) where you live—and whose house it used to be, 5) and how much you paid for the house. I swear, there are no secrets in a small town.

What happens when healthcare's own gets hurt or ill? I very much respect HIPAA, but when one of our close team members or their immediate family comes into our small hospital's ED with a devastating illness or injury, suddenly some of us *happen* to wander through the ED, willing to help out. A few years ago, the ED doc called me and said, "You're on call, right? I can't tell you anything, but you need to get over here right now." My practice partner's spouse had suddenly passed away in the ED and my partner was alone and distraught. So yes, I dropped what I was doing to go be with them until we could get additional support. No way am I letting a colleague go through something like that alone if I can help it.

The Breakup Festival? It's not a true festival—I made

that part up. But there is the Dawson City Yukon Ice Pool, where anyone can buy tickets to place a bet on when the Yukon River will start flowing again. There are strict rules and precise measurements of the breakup moment. When I read about the event, I used it as the inspiration for my Yukon Valley Breakup Festival!

Somewhere in this book, I hid the cheesy mission statement from a healthcare organization with which I worked in the past. Super proud of that Easter egg! If you find it, email me at jillian@jilliandavid.net and tell me the statement. If you get it right, I'll send you a gift*!

(*The gift will *not* be a packet of hospital procedures and policies, I promise!)

Acknowledgments

Big thanks to my vascular surgery colleague, HL, who calmly answered all of my increasingly disturbing questions about a femoral artery laceration and how to repair it at bedside. I'm sure the thought of a non-OR repair by a non-surgeon horrified him. I did have to explain that I didn't have any bodies in the basement, that he knew of ...

Thank you to fabulous editor Julie Sturgeon, who pulls amazing feats of writing out of me that I didn't know were possible.

Lastly, this book is dedicated to the hospice teams who have ministered to my patients and their families over the years. I am blessed to have worked side-by-side in such challenging and meaningful situations. Thank you for the hard work and compassionate care you provide.

If you enjoyed *Paging Dr. Breakup*,
you'll love the other books in the…

The Yukon Valley, Alaska Series

Book 1: *Dr. Alaska*

Book 2: *Paging Dr. Breakup*

Book 3: *Five Alarm Love*

Available now at your favorite online retailer!

About the Author

Award-winning and bestselling author Jillian David quickly writes then slowly edits medical romance, paranormal romance, and romantic suspense books. She loves to use medical situations and characters to drive drama in her books. Her favorite cell is the platelet and her least-favorite organ is the pancreas. She fully believes that curse words, when appropriately deployed during surgery, are hemostatic. Which also explains why no book of hers will ever bleed out...

Thank you for reading

Paging Dr. Breakup

If you enjoyed this book, you can find more from all our great authors at TulePublishing.com, or from your favorite online retailer.